Crooked

An Anthology of New Crime and Thriller Writing

Crooked Holster

Editing & typesetting: Jo Young, Sandra Kohls
Cover photography: Shanna L. Maxwell; SparkyInk photography
Cover design: Brenda Engberts Kaya

ISBN-13: 978-1519267610
ISBN-10: 1519267614

Contents

Crooked Holster

Ritual

FOREWORD

What turns people to a life of writing crime? Is it the high stakes, sex, violence and chance to vicariously carry a pistol? Crime writing embraces jeopardy. It sets the blood pumping faster through the reader's veins, but the best of the genre is composed of more than a series of violent thrills.

The crime genre, like all good writing, depends on convincing characterisation. Readers may find some protagonists challenging or even downright nasty, but they have to be curious about what will happen to them, or the book is a dud. Crime writers are often exploring lives that have been set off kilter, people who are somehow at odds with society. Many of our stories are quests. They follow the progress of someone searching for the solution to a crime, which in turn sets them on a geographical journey. Good crime fiction is more than a trip predicated by a MacGuffin. It transports the reader into the margins of society, to places where they may not wish to travel, except on the page.

Even when it is set in the past, good crime writing is an expression of the period in which it is written. Writers are not equipped to find solutions to society's problems, but they have a knack for identifying popular concerns. At its worse, this tendency can slip into literary vampirism, the writer sucking up outrage in the hope of high book sales. But when it works, it results in socially engaged fiction which helps us to see the world and its problems in ways we may not have conceived.

I love crime fiction because it is the whole package. Good writing, brilliant characterisation, sharp observation and a twist turning story that keeps me reading. The writers in Crooked Holster love the genre too. They have created an anthology that will keep you turning the page and will leave you with a different aspect on the world. Hold onto your hats!

Louise Welsh
Glasgow 2015

Knox and the Hate Mail

David McVey

The Revd. Melville Knox's most irritating quality was his habit of turning up at my office unannounced. A former research zoologist now in the Church of Scotland ministry, he was often consulted by the police on crimes with a religious angle. He'd become used to disturbing the contemplative repose of a biochemistry academic at the University of South Glasgow - me - in order to secure an instant second opinion.

Actually, there was little of the dreaming spires about my job. I had paperwork, emails by the hundred, working groups, meetings, daft new 'initiatives' from the Government and, very occasionally, some lecturing. Being torn away from this was generally a good thing, except that I would, eventually, have to catch up.

Knox appeared in my office one September mid-morning when I was putting together the finishing touches to a pre-semester conference we were hosting.

'London?' I yelled, 'London? Do you know how busy I am, Knox? We have a conference coming up, it's Freshers' Week after that and... you don't seem to realise I'm in charge of this department!'

'Do you know, Malky,' said Knox, in his sonorous preaching voice, 'I often pray that you be freed from your spirit of churlish unhelpfulness.'

Within an hour we were settled in a train at Glasgow Central, about to leave for London. My plea for First Class seats had horrified Knox's Spartan instincts and so we were travelling cattle class with the screaming children, too-loud iPods and bellowing stag parties.

'You have heard of Dorothy Berkshire, a columnist on The Guardian?'

'Of course I have. You go on about her all the time. It's as if you fancy her.'

A cold stare was turned on me. 'Ms Berkshire is a leading secular liberal opinion former. She has been called a champagne socialist, though her socialism is not of a thoroughgoing nature. Her writing style only catches fire when she is expressing her irrational hatred of faith and religion.'

'So?'

'We are meeting her tonight. She has received a threatening letter and the Metropolitan Police have suggested that I talk to her and examine the letter. She is convinced that they have been sent by a crazed Christian who intends her harm.'

'So this is just another of your atheist-bashing expeditions, with me along to provide an audience?'

But Knox had already rested his head on the back of his seat, closed his eyes and descended into the sudden deep sleep he always claimed was a state of prayerful meditation. In the seats behind us, four drunks were noisily playing cards while across the aisle a boisterous family watched a noisy DVD on a laptop; their snottery-nosed toddler crawled towards me and drooled on my shoe. It would be a long journey.

Knox had arranged to meet Ms Berkshire in our hotel lounge. She was a striking, ash-blonde woman in her late 50s, conservatively dressed and coiffed. She turned a reserved but slightly smug grin on Knox, attired as usual in his black three-piece suit and clerical collar.

'I'm not sure what your role is in this business, Mr Knox,' she said in a warm RP voice like milky coffee. Knox might not fancy Dorothy Berkshire, but I was beginning to. 'However, the Met advised me to speak to you, and here I am.'

'It's Revd. Knox.' said Knox.

The ensuing silence was awkward, like an itch you couldn't reach, so I broke it, asking, 'Can I get you something to drink, Ms Berkshire?'

By the time we were comfortably settled with a large cafetiere and a selection of pastries, Knox had defrosted enough to introduce me ('Malcolm Kennedy, Professor of Biochemistry at a minor Scottish university...') and to ask about the letter Ms Berkshire had received.

'It came on Sept 2nd, a Wednesday. My column runs on a Monday, as you'll know, Mr Knox, and on 31st August I had taken a particularly critical standpoint with regard to the theists who still wield power in our secular society. The letter coming just two days later makes the connection rather obvious.'

'Ah, yes, I recall that article' said Knox, 'you write it rather often. Do you have a copy of this version available?' Ms Berkshire produced a smartphone, tapped and stroked the screen and handed it to Knox. 'It's still online,' she said.

Knox read and scrolled slowly, making occasional remarks under his breath and once breaking into harsh cold laughter. I began discussing the weather with Dorothy Berkshire to shield her from him.

When he had finished, Knox handed the phone back to Ms Berkshire and fell into sermonising. 'A most egregious piece, Miss Berkshire,' he began, 'though I see that I shall have to re-educate your understanding of some of the mechanisms of evolution as outlined in modern theories.' A stunned-looking Dorothy Berkshire made as if to speak but Knox dismissed her with a wave of the hand, as if she were a troublesome insect. 'So you assume,' he went on, 'that some simple believer was stung by this ill-researched attack on faith and religion into writing to you?'

'I think that's the most obvious conclusion, Mr Knox, don't you?'

Knox smiled. A grim sight. I always had to look away.

'Happily, Miss Berkshire, in my profession we are required often to look beyond the obvious to what is true.'

I was relieved when the discussion concluded, and Dorothy Berkshire left the hotel to be swallowed up by a waiting taxi; if she'd been a man she'd probably have belted Knox at some point. I know I would've.

'I take it back Knox; you don't fancy her.'

Knox sniffed. 'Anyway, Malky, what do you make of it?'

'Surely she's right? It's the most obvious motive.'

'Yes, Malky. Either the letter was sent by an aggrieved Christian believer angered by Miss Berkshire's column, or...'

'Or what?'

'Or there is some other explanation entirely. Come, now, let us investigate the dinner capabilities of this hotel and praise the Lord for his provision. Tomorrow morning we shall examine this remarkable threatening letter.'

Next morning we arrived at a police station on the edge of Central London. Inspector Harvey, a tired-looking CID officer, welcomed us and showed us into a small room furnished only with chairs and a formica table.

Harvey explained, 'A hand-written note, on plain paper, a bullet folded in newspaper, packaged in a used jiffy bag; all prior address labels, sender's labels and the like carefully removed. No prints on the bullet, which is standard issue, easily got hold of.'

'Hmm,' Knox mumbled, 'Sounds almost ritualistic, as if the person has done this before, or will do it again.'

'That's what we thought at first,' said Harvey, 'but we've heard of no other cases like this.'

'DNA?' said Knox.

'In a case like this, it's difficult to justify the cost of DNA testing. Of course, if the guy came back and physically attacked Ms Berkshire...'

'So it is not considered necessary to disburse

resources to prevent an attack,' said Knox, gravely, 'but some expenditure may be risked once he has actually harmed someone, prior perhaps to repeating the pattern?'

'Politicians, eh? Anyway, we don't know that this person is dangerous, yet.'

Knox examined the bullet, and then smoothed out the ragged shred of newspaper in which it had been wrapped. 'A local paper from the North of England,' he said.

I took it from him; the Penley Examiner. I asked Harvey, 'Have you made any enquiries in this Penley?'

'The population of the town is 80,000, not counting the surrounding countryside and villages. Where do you start?'

We looked at the jiffy bag and then Knox took up the letter. I looked over his shoulder and we read it together.

ITS ABOUT TIME SOME ONE SHUT
YOU UP YOU BITCH - WHAT YOU DONE
WONT NEVER BE FORGOT - I WISH I
CUD FIRE ONE OF THESE AT YOU

AND GET YOU RIGHT IN THE THROAT
SO YOU CUD DIE SLOW

Back outside, I scuttled to keep up with Knox's furious fundamentalist pace, as we made our way back to the hotel. Over lunch he said 'We must consider other angles, other people who may wish to harm Miss Berkshire for other reasons. What of her first husband? What of the people she has mixed with in politics and journalism? The secular establishment, you see, is all too keen to blame everything it can on 'fundamentalism' of a religious nature. Yet everyone is a fundamentalist about something.'

'What am I fundamentalist about, Knox?'

Knox gave me a withering glance. 'I do not know, Malky. There are bound to be exceptions.'

I trailed after Knox, towards the nearest academic library, feeling like the last non-fundamentalist, the last remaining person of no fixed convictions, in the entire world.

'This might all be pointless, Knox. My money is still on someone reading her Guardian column and sending off the letter in hot blood.'

I was at my laptop, the screen displaying the home page of the Penley Examiner - there were so many adverts it had taken about five minutes to load.

'How would you characterise a Guardian reader, Malky?' Knox was arching his bony frame over a table groaning with reference books, most of them open at the letter 'P'.

'Eh? What's that got to do with anything? I don't know... wealthy. Liberal. South-east England, mostly. University-educated.'

'Indeed, university-educated.' He continued browsing for a while and then turned to me and said, 'The threatening letter did not seem like one written by a stereotypical Guardian reader, did it?'

And of course he was right. Then he burst out, 'Ah! Here we are!'

'What is it?'

'Who do you think was the SDP candidate for Penley and Lower Lykedale in the 1983 General Election?'

'Pudsey the Bear. How do I know?'

He tutted, and said, 'Dorothy Berkshire. I knew the name 'Penley' had some connection with her. She polled less than 3000 votes, but took sufficient from the Labour candidate, Jack Handale, to ensure that the Conservative was elected.'

'So what? Some disgruntled ex-SDP official is threatening failed candidates from thirty-odd years ago? Hang on - Jack Handale?' I scrolled down the page on my screen. 'He's in this week's issue of the Examiner.'

'For what reason?'

'Because he's just died.'

Handale had been stricken with prostate cancer during the summer and had declined quickly, perishing in a local nursing home early in September. I read out a couple of paragraphs recounting his career as a panel beater, his rise to the upper levels of his trade union, and then his nine years as the local Labour MP. By the time I'd finished, some intensely-studious library users were throwing me dirty looks.

'So you think Handale might have decided to give our Dorothy one last fright before he went?'

'No, Malky. Handale appears to have been a man of some depth and integrity. This does not have his stamp - and he would have produced a more articulate letter. He must be part of the story, though. Could you find the home page of the nursing home involved?'

I did so, and passed the laptop to Knox.

'We go to Penley by the first train tomorrow, Malky...'

'No "we" don't, Knox. I have a department to run and a conference to convene. I have hundreds of new students arriving who, not unreasonably, want someone there to educate them.'

Next morning we both left from Euston, me on a Glasgow train, Knox bound for Lancashire. He clearly felt that he was about to make a breakthrough and was annoyed that no one would be there to witness his triumph. I didn't hear from him for a while and was surprised, on a Friday some weeks later, to receive a phone call inviting me to meet him in a Glasgow hotel. 'Miss Berkshire is recording a BBC Scotland programme today and is staying at the Royal Stewart afterwards. I have arranged to meet her to reveal the truth about her hate mail.'

'I haven't noticed anything in the papers.'

'It was only an isolated poison pen letter,

Malky, not the beginning of an ominous pattern. In any case, no one will be prosecuted.'

Another hotel lounge, another city; as I arrived, Dorothy Berkshire, fetching-looking as ever, was already listening to Knox at his most orotund. They both nodded to me but Knox didn't stop speaking.

'You see, clearly it was not a regular Guardian reader, but someone who had seen the paper on an isolated occasion. Tellingly, the writer upbraided you for what you 'done', not what you wrote. Jack Handale entered the nursing home just a few days before the column that concerns us. He took the Guardian, of course, and no doubt made comment on that Monday that here, glaring at him from the page, as she did every week, was his old nemesis. For after all, Miss Berkshire, the SDP effectively guaranteed the return of Mrs Thatcher's Conservatives, which I am sure was not your intent. As such, you have since promoted the myth of Labour's 'longest suicide note in history'. An explanation which does not, of course, hold water.'

'That's preposterous, Mr Knox, I...'

'Could we get back to the point, Knox?'

Knox smiled wickedly and continued. 'The people of Penley remember the Thatcher administration, the closure of their steelworks and the misery that ensued. They never forgave the London interloper who ensured they did not even have an articulate local representative to argue their case in Parliament. And when Mr Handale pointed your column out in the nursing home lounge, there were several voices raised in anger. "It's all right for her, she's still got her job down there in that London" was the general feeling.' Here, Knox had assumed a convincing Lancashire accent, which surprised me.

'And one of them sent the letter?' said Dorothy Berkshire.

'Yes. A fine old gentleman who was made redundant from the steelworks soon after the election. I visited him in his room, in which he has kept many relics of his time in the works, and also of his National Service days.'

'Bullets?' I asked.

'Among other memorabilia, yes.' said Knox. 'Of course, I do not intend to identify the sender, nor have I passed his details to the police. I have merely explained the situation to them and advised that no further proceedings be undertaken. The gentleman concerned is more sinned against than sinning.'

'Trust you to bring the Bible into it.'

Knox sighed heavily, sadly. 'That is not from the Bible, Malky. It is Shakespeare; King Lear.'

Dorothy Berkshire looked at Knox, at me, and then back at Knox again. Or perhaps she was just shaking her head. She looked like someone who was very keen to get back to London.

Peartree Road

Charlie Hughes

It's a quiet street, always has been.

From the corner with Banstead, down to where the Church interrupts the terraced houses, Peartree Road has become its own little community. For London, zone 2, it's quiet. No more than sixty homes and we all get along fine.

I stick close to home most of the time, so I see more of my neighbours than most. The only work I ever had was laying bricks, but Sammy Johnson and his wayward forklift saw to that. My leg still hurts like hell when the deep cold comes in January.

One of the nice things about Peartree Road is all the people who have the time to stop for a chat. Mrs. Trenton was one of those.

I'd known of her for most of my life, but we'd never really spoken. Her son Nigel was two ahead of me at school, so I'd see her waiting at the school gates, chatting with the other mums. She only moved to our end of Peartree Road a few years ago after her husband died.

I started to see her on the street and we got talking about all sorts: My bad leg, the dog shit lying about, the weather, anything really. She told me Nigel went to New Zealand to work for an engineering company. Apparently, he didn't call much and she'd only ever seen her grand-daughter twice. Terrible shame it was.

She'd trundle along Peartree Road with her rolling basket most days, making a big deal out of getting the newspaper every morning. Because I'm soft, I did what any kind-hearted person would do and paid her some special attention. Every other day I popped round for a cup of tea and a biscuit. I mended the pipe under her sink when it leaked. I kept a close eye on her comings and goings, just to make sure nobody was trying to take advantage.

The first couple of years she was here, that's all it was. Just me being a friendly neighbour, a good citizen, if you like. Then she started to get ill. Her breathing was never great, but it took a turn for the worse. The doctors told her the arteries in her lungs had blown up because of smoking. Emphysema. Mucus in her airways which she couldn't clear.

As time went by it got worse and worse. First she was on this little inhaler, no big deal. Then she moved onto some serious drugs which played merry hell with her sleep, until finally they gave her this Oxygen capsule strapped to set of wheels which she had to drag around the house with her.

Watching this happen was awful. I'd grown quite fond of the old girl. Over a period of six months, I watched a healthy seventy year-old fall to bits.

The mental side of things was the worst. The struggle she had gasping for air, all day every day. She stopped leaving the house and became more and more reliant on me. She didn't have anybody else. I'd get her shopping and pop in to see her twice a day. On the days when there weren't any 'meals on wheels', I'd make sure she got something to eat.

The council tried to foist some home-carer on her but we told them to get packing. It was no skin off my nose. I had all the time in the world and it was nice for me to have somebody to talk to. Only problem was, with her struggles, Mrs. Trenton started to develop a difficult side. She complained that I wouldn't "leave her be", even threatened to call the police. It always depended on what mood you got her in.

I got a copy of her key made, so I could let myself in. Save her getting up and struggling to the door every time I came by. She didn't like it too much at first. Said she was going to get the locks changed, but she never did.

To make a point, I left her on her own for a couple of days. When I finally returned, she was sat on the floor, clutching her oxygen mask, in little pool of her own piss. I got her up and cleaned her off, bathed her and got her into bed. She managed a 'Thank you' before she drifted off to sleep. Gent that I am, I resisted the temptation to ask if I was intruding.

It all happened pretty quickly after that. Social services came round a couple of times when I was there. I told them I was her son. It was easier that way because nobody would have believed I was helping out of the kindness of my own heart. It's surprising how easily people will believe stuff like that. Even when Mrs. Trenton told the young social worker I wasn't even related to her, all I had to do was tap the side of my head with my finger. The kid just nodded.

You know what she said to me? Something terrible, horrible lies. An outburst which seemed to come from nowhere.

I'd just come in from the shops and was putting the cans away in the kitchen cupboard. She stood in the doorway, and started talking.

'I remember you Tommy, when you were a little one. I never told you about this before because I thought you might be offended. But now we're so close n' all, what's the harm?' She wheezed and took on some oxygen.

'Must have been around '71, maybe '72. I'd picked up my Nigel from school and took him home and put tea on. I was in the kitchen when he came up to me and says "Mum, I lost my scarf. I think I dropped it at school." So I put tea in the oven and dropped Nigel with a neighbour. I rushed back to the school.' She wheezed again and gave an odd little smile, like she was secretly pleased about something.

'You know what I saw as I walked into the school gates? You. Just stood there in your tatty little jacket. Couldn't have been more than five years old. I don't know where the teachers were. Well, my heart broke for you, stood there, all alone. "Hello Tommy," I said. "Where's your mummy?" You didn't say a word. Poor little thing. You just started crying, quietly, like you didn't want me to see.' She smiled again. The old bag took another hit of oxygen and continued.

'I tried to do the right thing. I knew where you lived, not because my Nigel had ever been round to play. But because there was all that talk when the police had been called. Some row between your Mum and Dad. Everyone knew about it. When we got to your house, your mum answered the door. I was just waiting for her to thank me, to give me some excuse about why she'd forgotten to pick you up. Not a bit of it. "What are you doing with my son?" she screamed. "Get in this house you little shit." She grabbed your arm and dragged you into the hallway. Then she turned to me and said. "You can take that smug look off your face. I was just on my way to get him." Well,

I was stunned. I'd never heard such language from a woman. You remember what a horrible cow your Mum was?'

Of course, I didn't say anything. I just kept on packing the groceries away. It's one thing to know that old, frail people can turn vicious and spiteful, but it's quite another to see it for yourself.

It was only two days later that we had our little incident. I'd let myself in as usual, popped my head round the corner and saw her sat there wheezing away on the sofa. 'Fancy a cup of Cocoa?' I asked.

'Why don't you leave me alone?'

'I'll take that as a no then!' I said, teasing her.

After I'd put the milk on the stove, I came back to the front room and sat next to her on the sofa. She was watching Newsnight. Well, I've never been a fan of the news so I ask her if it's okay for me to turn it over.

'Why can't you leave me alone?' she says again, but this time she was more upset. She put her oxygen mask to her face and took a hit.

'I'm helping you Mrs. Trenton. You know that.'

'You're not helping me. You're using me! Eating all my food and telling social services I don't need any help. It's evil. It's wrong.' She wheezed heavily again and took in more from her mask.

I just ignored her. She was in one of her nasty moods again. I got up and turned the telly over, thinking a bit of Graham Norton might lighten the mood. Not a bit of it.

Hacking and wheezing she could only just speak. 'Your time's up.' She said. 'I'm not taking your nonsense anymore. Tomorrow morning, I'm calling the police. Your mother was right. You are a little shit.'

She noticed my reaction. Somehow, all in an instant, she knew more than she was ever supposed to. Wheezing still, she managed a smile and then said it again, louder, more slowly this time. 'You're . . . a . . . little . . . shit.' It was a screechy, shrill.

So I got up. Hand on my heart, I was going to leave, but she started to go into one of her coughing fits. I waited. The wheezing was getting worse. She sounded like a kettle coming to the boil and then turning itself off, over and over again.

Mrs. Trenton reached for her oxygen mask and that was when I made my decision. All in an instant, I knew what I had to do for this woman. Here she was, struggling just to get from one day to the next. Struggling to breathe for heaven's sake! And it was turning her nasty, it was making her hate the world and the only person in it who cared for her.

I pulled the little oxygen tank away from her and, in turn, the mask slipped out of her hand, tumbling across the floor. She didn't do anything to chase it.

'Please. . .' she said, quietly. Then she started coughing again, this time more violently. Each time she tried to suck in more air you could hear the airways closing up. I've heard people say 'so-and-so turned blue' many times and never really thought much of it. Well, apparently there's some truth in it. The purple-blue veins on her neck and cheeks bulged out, colouring her.

It took another couple of minutes for the struggling to stop. She fell forward onto the floor, grasping for the oxygen. I stood for a while, just watching to see if she was breathing. When I was sure, I went into the kitchen and turned off the milk, most of which had bubbled over onto the stove. I rinsed out the pan and put on some more.

Once I'd had my drink I went back into the front room, turned off the telly and sat down on the sofa. Mrs. Trenton's body was still slumped in the same position. I took off one of my gloves and put my palm on her back. She was still warm, but it was fading.

By that point I'd been looking after Mrs. Trenton for almost three years. Day in and day out I'd been doing my bit, usually for very little thanks and often for lots of abuse. I'd never received a penny from her for my troubles.

She had about eight grand in her account, I'd known that for a while. She'd been squirrelling it away over the years on the off-chance Nigel would invite her out to New Zealand.

I got her purse from the mantelpiece and removed the debit card. I knew the PIN by heart from the shopping trips. Of course, before, she'd always said she was checking the withdrawals, making sure I wasn't taking any liberties. There wasn't much danger of that anymore.

I made sure the curtains were tightly drawn, watched telly for a couple of hours and then left, locking the door behind me.

Over the next three weeks I emptied the account, including the overdraft. I had seven places around Camberwell and Peckham which I reckoned were poorly covered by CCTV. They were all cheap-looking cash points, the robbing type that make you pay £1.75 for the privilege of accessing your money.

I knew I'd have some breathing space, but I got lucky. Would you believe, it took them nine months before anyone found her. The council bailiffs broke in because the rent hadn't been paid. There was a bit of a stink when her beloved Nigel found out the bank account was bare. The police even came to see me because some nosy fucker mentioned I'd been hanging around her. They had nothing and I knew it.

So here I am, fine and dandy. Still got seven grand tucked away in the attic. Still making the time to keep an eye on the old ones as they come and go.

I notice Mrs. Tiverton from number 73 is struggling a bit these days.

Golden Brown

Ellis Goodwin

I like golden brown, I like the way it moves into the glass. It's silk sliding off a woman's thigh or diving into a warm Caribbean sea. It's not that I don't drink when I'm on a case but the golden brown I keep till the end.

That molten mellow fire is my reward for being a smart ass shit stirrer and for knowing what to do when it all rises to the surface. I unlock the draw and take out my crystal tumbler. It sparkles slightly and you can see tiny rainbows through the cut glass. That's what she used to like, the rainbows in my glass, not the hard stuff I pour into it.

I look at the chip on the top, just to remind me, then let the sweet stuff bless the inside. I take that first sip, chip towards me, pressing against my lower lip. It slides down, corroding my throat, setting fire to my empty belly, warming and soothing my jangled parts.

My whole body sighs down to my toes.

There's some dirty Jazz seeping up from the club below and the whole room seems to sway with it's naughty rhythm. I'm just ready for the next sip when I see a shadow creeping up to the frosted glass on my office door. The shadow pulls back an uncertain hand to knock.

'Come in,' I say before she, the shadow looks like a she, has a chance to knock. Jesus I really am a smart ass.

'Hello?' says the shadow.

'Come in,' I say again. This time with a little more gruff to my voice. It's after midnight and I have a lot of drinking to do before the sun starts showing off.

She enters and a concerto of a woman walks in, hold the brass but heavy on violins. I look at her fresh face and can't shake the feeling that she's on the way to teach the Von Trap children. She looks like she's in a parade representing spring.

Then she smiles and I see a kind of wickedness playing on those lips. The kind I like. I start to tingle. To much drink or not enough? I take another slow sip to steady myself and try not to look at her curves as she settles in the chair opposite me.

She smooths her dress down over her knees and I know I'm already swept up in her. Carried away in her tide. What the hell is wrong with me? Fixing me with her baby blues, she smiles again, this time she's more nervous and her tongue quickly traces her top lip.

I take a slug from the glass. All form and routine forgotten. 'Mr Dant,' she says, 'I'm in trouble.'

'This would be a strange place to be if you weren't.' Better, throw a little distance in between you. Build a wall and hope she doesn't touch her thigh and bring it crumbling down again.

She pauses as if lifting a heavy burden off of herself, 'A very bad man wants me dead Mr Dant. I want you to kill him for me.'

Okay so now I'm back.

Now I'm looking at this from a thousand different angles. Little Miss Sweet-Cheeks is still throwing me the innocent sultry pout but I've suddenly sobered up.

This just got interesting.

Feeling Safe

Laura R. Becherer

The courthouse bells across the square began to ring, and Lucy looked up from the thin volume of Petrushevskaya love stories on her lap. She stood up, her knees cracking from sitting so long on the wooden stool behind the counter, and lighted the lamp on the glass case next to her. It lent a shadowy light to the room and illuminated the dust motes that floated in the air.

Lev, her black lab, lifted his head from the dusty floor and looked at her.

'It's okay,' she said. 'Stay, Lev.' Lev lay his head back down, and Lucy began her shop-closing rounds. The towers of mismatched volumes were intimidating in this biting cold that the rusted hot water heating system couldn't cure.

Lev yawned. He was almost hidden, his black fur melting into the dark floor except where it gleamed in the lamplight. His brown eyes shone, though, and they followed Lucy's hands as she counted the money and tucked it under the drawer.

Lucy locked the till. No one had come in for the last hour and Lev wasn't disturbed, so there was nothing to worry about. Still, it was her job to check.

Lucy began on the ground floor, walking round the history and biography cases before heading up the wooden stairs, past the row of antique books to the loft and back room above. Self help was empty, as was crime and western and the children's books room in the far corner. It was warmest in here, and Lucy took a moment to rub her fingerless-mittened hands above the radiator before heading back downstairs. A muffled thud echoed from the darkest corner of the loft when she was halfway down the stairs; Lucy jumped and clutched the banister, trying to steady her breathing.

'There was no one there,' she told herself. 'You just checked. It's okay. Look at Lev—he's not worried.' Lev had picked up his head again and twitched, but now he lay back down, calm.

'No one is back there,' Lucy said to Lev. She took a deep breath and forced herself to turn around and go check. A book had slipped off a crowded shelf and landed on the floor. She picked it up and put it back, but she couldn't shake the feeling that someone was watching her. A spasm of fear made her spin around, peering into the gloomy hall. Nothing.

'It's fine,' she told herself again, but as she headed back across the landing to the stairs she noticed that her hands were shaking.

This bookstore was Lucy's favorite place in the world, but she was eager, at least for tonight, to get out of it. She tucked her book back into her satchel and pulled on her grey pea coat, buttoning it snugly before winding a red woollen scarf around her neck and pulling a matching beanie onto her head, taking care to tuck every strand of pink pixie out of sight. Lucy took one last look around the store and turned out the lamp, then took Lev's leash out of her pocket and clipped it to his collar. Together they hurried across the room to the door, which jangled as Lucy wrenched open the frozen handle and closed it behind her.

Lucy hated turning her back to the street while she locked the old-fashioned door, even though Lev was right beside her as a guard, but she did it as quickly as she could and spun around again to face the lamp lit street. Snow covered the sidewalks and the tops of her leather boots, already numbing her toes. Small snowflakes, glittering white and fresh in the lamplight, drifted down to the pavement. It was almost Christmas—the lights on the square cheerfully illuminated the shops. It was only early evening, but darkness fell so fast during Midwestern winters that it felt more like midnight. Classic carols hummed from the speakers set around the square.

Lucy took a deep breath of cold, clean winter air. The snow was beautiful but bitter when flung by the wind against her face. She tugged on Lev's leash and they set off.

Lucy relaxed a little as they walked. The winter river rushed through the night-time, sounding louder and colder than it did in the day. They paused to stare at the turbulent blackness dotted glints of city lights. It was snowing harder now, the flakes grown fluffy and soft. They spun their ballerina skirts down to the river water and stuck to Lucy's eyelashes.

'Like the Sugarplum Fairy,' Lucy said to Lev,

who was snuffling at a tree trunk. A splash came from the river, which made Lucy jump but Lev bark and try to jump after it.

'Stop!' Lucy laughed, clinging to his leash and turning her back to the street to pull him back. 'Stop, you great big idiot, you can't go swimming in the middle of December. Lev, hold *still*, you nut.'

'Need some help?' a voice asked behind her.

Lucy gasped as she turned around, digging one hand into her coat pocket to find her mace. Lev stopped trying to bound into the river and barked sharply, trotting up to stand between Lucy and the man who was in front of her: a tall, gangly man in a dark parka and a wooly blue beanie. Lucy looked closely at his face—no, it wasn't Dorian.

'No thanks,' she said, trying to sound calm, but she knew she sounded unfriendly and short. She unclutched the mace in her palm and took her hand out of her pocket to pick up Lev's leash again.

'Look, sorry to scare you.' He held both hands in the air. 'Just trying to help, babe.' He walked away.

Lucy clenched Lev's leash in her hand; the dog quieted and pressed his warm side against her legs. Lucy knelt on the ground and put her arms around him; he licked her face.

'Thanks, bud,' she said. 'Let's just go home, okay? Mom will be calling soon, anyway.'

Lucy unlocked the outer door and climbed the stairs to her apartment, stopping to unlock the two new deadbolts in addition to the door handle. Lev then accompanied her as she checked every corner of the apartment. She opened closet doors, looked in the shower, peered under the bed with a flashlight. Lev stuck his nose in the closet and sniffed, then looked at Lucy.

'All clear,' she said, and went to the kitchen to get a slice of cold pizza and her bottle of Icelandic vodka, pausing to turn up the heat a few notches before settling in the living room. White French doors opened inward to separate the living room and bedroom from the rest of the apartment. Lucy bolted the doors closed at the top and then dragged the coffee table in front of them.

'There,' she said. Lev thumped his tail on the carpet in agreement.

Lucy checked to make sure the blinds were

closed and then turned on the coffee table lamp and the Christmas tree lights, which lit across the white walls to create a multicolored glow. She flicked the stereo on as well; Celtic Christmas music warmed the room, not so loud that she couldn't easily hear over it.

Lucy flopped over on the couch, facing the glass doors, and pulled a scratchy blanket over her knees. She had just poured herself a glass of vodka when her phone rang.

'Home for the night?' her mother asked when she answered.

'Yeah, I just got in,' Lucy said. 'There was a weird thing with a guy at the river, but it turned out to be nothing.'

'Luce, I wish you wouldn't walk down there,' her mother said. 'It's like you're trying to pick a secluded spot.'

'I'm not,' Lucy said. 'Lev likes it down there, is all, and it's so pretty and calming.'

'Lucy.'

'I know, I know. Mom, I'm trying.'

'I know,' her mom sighed. 'Hug Lev for me, okay? Are your doors locked?'

'Locked, double-locked, bolted, and I'm barricaded in the living room,' Lucy said. 'I should be good.'

'Well, be safe. Call me if you need anything.'

'Thanks, Mom,' Lucy hung up and tossed the phone on the couch and reached behind her sofa to plug it into her charger. She positioned the phone so that it was only six inches from her reach. Lev jumped up onto the sofa and curled up at her feet as small as a 70-pound dog could.

'*За нашу дружбу*!' Lucy toasted him with her vodka glass, then opened her satchel to her Petrushevskaya, along with her overstuffed Moleskine and her fountain pen so she could make dissertation notes. A deep sip of vodka burned her throat pleasantly and spread a warmth down her arms and legs into her weather-chilled fingertips and goes. A mandolin and flute sang *In the Bleak Midwinter* through the room as Lucy read and wrote, chewing on her lip ring and ruffling her spiky hair with one hand while Lev puppy-snored at her feet.

By one o'clock in the morning, Lucy was asleep in her clothes with her book draped across her stomach and her notebook on the floor. Lev still snored, his sleek fur glowing in the comforting Christmas lights. The CD was on repeat; '*O Come O Come Emmanuel*' was now crooning in a low, eerie tone echo.

Suddenly, Lev sat up, tense and on guard. He barked, loud and urgent. Lucy sat up in abrupt sleepy terror and confusion, her hair sticking up in the back and her contacts dry in her eyes. Lev barked again, then jumped off the couch to stand in front of the living room doors, growling.

'What is it?' Lucy whispered to Lev, grabbing for her phone and holding a finger over the emergency button. Lev stopped growling for a moment, and then Lucy heard it—the scratching, and the faint jiggle of the door handle.

'Jesus Christ.' Lucy flung her book aside as she tumbled off the couch and knocked over the vodka bottle on the way to her room. Lev followed close behind. Lucy bundled herself inside the closet on the floor, calling 911 as she did so. She closed the door almost all the way, leaving only a sliver so that she could see Lev standing in front of it, fur bristling.

'911 Operator, what is your emergency?' said the cool voice on the other end of the line.

'Hello, my name is Lucy Cormany and I live at 1215 South Dewey Street,' Lucy whispered. 'Someone's breaking into my apartment, apartment number eleven. Help me, help me please.'

'Ma'am, slow down,' the dispatcher said with the practiced calm that Lucy knew too well. 'Stay on the line with me, all right? I'm sending an officer now. Where are you?'

'I'm on the floor in my bedroom closet,' Lucy said, beginning to cry. She could feel a panic attack building in her chest.

'Okay, Lucy, just stay with me,' the dispatcher said. 'Just stay on the line with me, and keep talking. You're sure someone's breaking in?'

'Yes,' Lucy whispered, taking deep, practiced breaths and chewing on her sweater sleeve as she rocked back and forth. 'I heard it.'

'Okay, just stay calm,' the dispatcher said. 'Just stay with me, Lucy. We have an officer on his way now.'

Lucy stopped biting her sleeve and began

rubbing her palm against her thigh as she rocked back and forth faster. The closet was stuffy and she had the heel of a stiletto digging into her ass. She shifted back farther, so that she was hidden behind her longest wool cardigans in the farthest corner of the closet. Lev paced and the dispatcher soothed as Lucy put her head between her knees and choked her way through the panic.

It seemed like hours but was probably only fifteen minutes before the officer knocked at the door. The dispatcher confirmed that it was the officer at the door, and Lucy hung up. She coaxed herself out of the closet and crept to the front door, dragging away the coffee table and unbolting the living room doors first. Lev stayed close.

'Officer Hardy here. Open please, ma'am.'

Shaking, Lucy unlocked and opened the door, keeping it on the chain.

'Your badge, please?' she whispered. He held it out. She unchained the door and let him inside.

'What makes you sure it was your ex-boyfriend?' Officer Hardy asked her again a half an hour later. They were sitting in the living room, still tree-lit and softened by Christmas music, although now the scene felt lurid and fake.

Lucy shook her head, taking another shaky sip of the water the officer had insisted she drink to 'calm down' before she gave a statement. She felt dizzy and slightly high, as she often did after a panic attack.

'Who else would it be?' she asked. 'He follows me, calls, texts, emails, leaving stuff on my doorstep—only my mother even knows that I live here! I know it was him.'

'You considered changing phone numbers? Getting a restraining order?'

'I did! I have one!' Lucy didn't mean to sound as angry as she felt. 'I have a restraining order. New phone. New city, even—I just moved here last month.'

'Well, unfortunately we can't do anything else unless he actually breaks in or attacks you,' Officer Hardy said. 'There's no way to prove he was here tonight. You sure you weren't just dreaming?' Lucy saw him eye the vodka bottle on the floor next to the couch. Her anger flared.

'No,' she said. 'Lev heard him, didn't you,

Lev?' She ruffled Lev's head. 'He woke me up, and I heard it. He was rattling the door handle.'

'Well, you seem to be well-protected here,' Officer Hardy said, looking around the room. 'Three locks on the door, another on the inside, and a nice big dog to keep you safe. Even if he was here tonight, he didn't get in. I think you'll be all right. Try to get some sleep. Call if anything happens.' He handed Lucy his card.

She thanked him dully, and he left. Lucy relocked all the doors, repositioned the coffee table, and went into her room. Lev followed.

Lucy stripped and slid on sweatpants and a sweatshirt. Lev jumped up and curled at the foot of the down comforter. Lucy shut the bedroom door and wedged her nightstand in front of it. She considered calling her mother, but it was after two in the morning.

'People can only take so much," she said to Lev, settling into bed. "Maybe we should ask for a lock for the bedroom door, too.'

Lev wiggled his way up the bed and rested his chin on Lucy's chest. She petted him and stared at the shadows her nightlight made on the ceiling. Christmas music still thrummed from the living room, an empty lullaby. It would be a long, long time before she fell asleep again.

Mud in the Vein

Christopher P. Mooney

You choose junk only once. After that it chooses you. When the habit's been formed, you have to have it and you'll do anything to get it. I took my first taste almost fourteen years ago and it's since become my way of life. I could say I started on it during a personal crisis or to cope with the horrors of grief but the truth is I had got bored with the usual pills and powders and was looking for the next big thing. I thought I'd found that in junk. After the long years of sordid routine, it's true to say I am where I am because of nothing more than dumb curiosity. Wondering about the unknown has cost me the whole lot.

Uncle Hugo's is a hustlers' dive that never shuts. Dawn until dusk you'll find every type of character in there. Mere shades among shadows, they're either propped up against the long walnut bar or huddled in a corner booth carving up the latest piece of work. Pimps and their hookers. Pushers and their addicts. Ex-cons. Careerists with eyes and ears open for a wheelman or an alibi. Bop musicians and vagabond poets washing down the remnants of broken dreams with warm lager served in a bottle or a glass. Even the occasional narcotics detective with his hand out. It's run by Irish Pat, a stocky man of fifty with enormous hands and a concrete face. Pat knows his customers and he knows the score. He also knows how to use a shotgun.

Pat's pouring drinks for me and Terry Snark, a double leech who'd sell you cancer if it meant a grain for him in return. Terry's a small-time jive artist who lives in a cold-water apartment near the meat-packing district. A more loathsome character never drew breath. I've got to be careful what I say because the word is he went wrong and is working with the authorities. Terry's tall and thin with long fingers dripping from bony hands. He's been in this game longer than most – having got his habit more than three decades ago – and has that look: shifty fish eyes sunk back behind protruding cheekbones that are covered with sallow flesh. The story of a hard life is etched across the parchment of his face. His mouth droops at the corners, giving him an imbecilic expression. When he's junk sick, the skin on his arms and legs twitches; as if in their desperation the junk-hungry cells are trying to burst out of his body in search of a fix. At these times, Terry won't bathe or change his clothes; claiming the water hurts him. He doesn't eat or sleep; using the little energy he has left to score. He doesn't have the sand to roll soaks on the subway so mooches about for half a cap on credit from the latest connection or from any of the other users he thinks might be holding, either here in the bar or outside the all-night cafeteria at the corner of Yardley Avenue whose food is tolerable only to people who don't taste what they put in their mouth.

This is what he's doing while I sip the dregs of a weak rum-coke, pestering me to let him have a share of the gear he imagines is stashed in my coat. On the cuff, of course. I tell him straight I don't have any. Hearing the answer is no and hearing I mean it, he falls silent; the thin lips of his rictus mouth set hard as stone. With no chance of getting a hit, there's nothing left to say. Terry's not here to socialise. I move round and watch him shuffle out onto the street.

I turn back to the bar and notice a hooker settling onto a stool across from me, all concentration-camp hips and deflated AlloDerm lips. She cracks open a benny tube and takes out the folded strips of paper. These she mixes crudely into a cup of black coffee, swallowing it all in one huge gulp. Within minutes she's checked out, a goofy beatific grin plastered across the rough contours of her face.

And still I wait.

'Are you anywhere?' he asks.

'No. You?'

'There's a panic on. I don't know nobody who's holdin'.'

'Can't you hook me up, man?' I push, trying to keep the urgency out my voice. 'I've got the dough.'

'How much you got?'

'Enough to put me right before the sickness starts.'

'Yeah?'

'Yeah. Tell me where.'

This city in the early hours reminds me of the dawn streets of my childhood with its brown-stone buildings caked with grime and putrid semen that's trodden on by barefoot bastards starved for attention with guts swollen on lard. The silver escalator with illiterate obscenities scrawled on its filthy damp walls reeks of the wanton poverty of take-away vomit and alcohol piss.

I find the right door and knock hard.

I get out my works and cook up, feeding my arm from the bloodied spike.

The familiar effects are instantaneous: first a hint behind the knees, then a warm feeling that washes all over the body. I'm soon lost in the foggy pursuit of fugitive meaning under a moon of blood in the quivering, quaking night.

When I wake up I've no idea where I am. Thick darkness and naked madness are everywhere and all around me.

I get four codeine tablets out my pocket and dissolve them in half a quart of milk I find in the refrigerator.

In the bathroom I resist the urge to vomit dry bile onto cracked porcelain. I look in the mirror. My face is red and hard like tenement bricks.

I roll up my shirt sleeve, put on my coat and leave.

A murder of crows stands in black silence under a heavy rain that's pounding the streets and flooding the gutters. I see intoxicated juveniles turning tricks for gas money under yellow street lamps as the uniforms drive by with bored looks and coffee cups.

I get my bearings and begin the long walk home.

The Motel Room

Olga Dermott-Bond

Your love flickers, like a headache of half-light,
Encased. Your smile designed to keep me out,
Like a cheap neon strip. Truth spreads at night,
Blooms like blood, a stain of darkening blood.
Afterwards, as always, you leave our hushed crime,
Evening lies mangled on static sheets, face down.
I am that twitching corpse, who wants more time -
Wants to tell someone *it was us*. Cover blown.
But, the taste of you thickens in my mouth,
My thrill now, only, an electric shock,
Your touch, a dull flutter of pain, a drought
Of longing. I should leave, but I'm your moth.

I lie, covers pulled tight over my mistakes,
Walls hum of paper-thin alibis I create.

Wash Away my Guilt

Robert White

I once washed my hands 200 times in a single day. The skin was so raw my hands swelled and cracked open at the tips like pistachios. The doctor told my parents that Xanax would help but all that did was leave me half-stoned squatting in a corner of my darkened bedroom contemplating ways I could kill myself least painfully.

I grew up. I stopped the incessant handwashing. But you know how it is if you know something about people. Whatever that obsessive compulsion was all about, it didn't go away altogether; it merely buried itself for a while like a bug in a cocoon and came out later in another form.

Even worse, I managed to aggravate that mental condition with another kind of self-inflicted mind fuck: I grew deeply religious in my post-adolescent years. While my friends were all going out clubbing, getting drunk or high and having easy sex with their Extasy pickups at raves, I was either in my same upstairs room at home or else in my dorm on my knees praying to a wrathful God and begging forgiveness for—what? I never quite knew, but I knew that I was the lowest, most worthless creature to draw breath. I conjured nightly visions of hell and, pathetic to admit, I sometimes masturbated to those dire images of millions of souls screaming in agonizing pain all around me in the fires of hell. It grew so weird that the more I ejaculated in my frenzied guilt, the more often I felt I needed to do this to assuage whatever masochistic desires were tormenting me.

I found relief in one thing only. I walk the streets at night—often in the still hours before dawn when everyone sleeps. I sometimes look in people's windows to see what their lives are like because I'm constantly seeking and failing to find an answer to why I can't fit into normalcy so I call myself a voyeur of normal people's lives. I could never explain this to a cop if I were seen peeping, but people undressed or having sex has only the slightest prurient interest for me. I'm after something else. I want an explanation from God, from somebody, how it is I'm here with no answers to the big questions.

Before my night walks, I was close to suicide. I'm a contemporary John Bunyan Pilgrim—and I still have Dante's hell to look forward to. The Roman Catholicism drilled into my childish brain the terror of hell's stinking sulphur pit of flames and a massive clock (the blue nuns said) tolling its single dire message: You'll never get out, you'll never get out—for all eternity.

One night changed it all. I noticed lights on in the house at the end of Treelane Drive about two miles from my house. A Porterhouse steak and mashed potatoes went untouched as if it were a steaming pile of garbage riddled with maggots.

The lights drew me, an anorectic moth to a flame. I moved from one patch of shadow to the next until I found myself standing in the backyard.

Three lit windows beckoned. I moved toward them mindful of tripping sensors. Sudden illumination spotlighting me has sent me scuttling back into the dark before on my outings. Nothing besides a dog barking a street away.

I hoisted myself by my fingertips on the window ledge. I never expect to see serial killers polishing knives or terrorists wiring fuses to pressure-cooker bombs or drug traffickers stuffing money into garbage bags—that's Hollywood fantasy. Nor do I expect to catch my double, a doppelgänger, gaping back at me. That's Poe or Dostoevsky.

Instead, I saw a room dedicated to Frank Sinatra. Every square inch of space and shelving filled with Sinatra memorabilia: posters, framed performance tickets, a trio of bobblehead dolls, even a life-sized mannequin with a checkered fedora circa 1950's. I had to do about ten of these "pullups" to see everything inside. How long I stared into this avid Sinatra fan's sanctum sanctorum I cannot recall. But it was like looking into the maw of my own personal hell. I imagined what it would be like to be tied to a chair in that room forced to hear an endless loop of Sinatra tunes. Svidrigailov's image of hell as a small filthy cottage with spiders in the corners was nothing to mine.

I left for my house in a state of numb shock. I understand hero worship and sports fanaticism as tribal impulses surviving from our limbic brain. This vision, however, disturbed me in a profound way. Whatever matrices collided in my head did not produce humor or contempt as might have happened in another. I found myself seething for revenge on Old Blue Eyes' biggest fan.

All the next day I moped about trying to scratch an itch. It was like having fiberglass particles in your clothes that drove you mad. Was Sinatra Man one of Goethe's "contented pigs"? I wanted to come back that night and hurl a Molotov cocktail through that triptych of window panes and burn his treasures.

My insomnia and OCD worsened. I avoided Treelane Drive as if it were radioactive ground. I had to touch the bark of certain trees on my nightly wanderings. I had to cross a certain street directly over a specific manhole cover. The repetitiveness of these tasks grew more daunting and more time-consuming. I would drop into bed exhausted. Sinatra Man's room was the first thought in my head and the last thought at dawn.

I had regressed back to the time my girlfriend dumped me. She was in my head continually as if her image had been impressed into my brain by a laser engraving machine. I once had to pull onto a freeway shoulder because that photo of her face was impossible to stop seeing. It took a long time to get back on my feet, but when I did, I discovered those childhood habits and tics had come back with a vengeance.

The Sinatra Man was one snowflake too many; the mountain side was coming down in a big avalanche unless . . .

Then I knew what had to be done. It would take meticulous planning, every dollar I had in my checking and savings accounts, and some luck to pull it off.

I went online to learn how to make a night-vision camera of my smart phone. I scoured memorabilia websites and e-Bay. I ordered a special-sized mannequin from a department store supply outlet.

Then I learned Sinatra Man's habits. That meant daytime surveillance, and because this wasn't my neighborhood, I could make only so many passes down this working-class street before somebody would remember me. But the same forces of darkness that forced me to walk through a Slough of Despond were now assisting me.

He was a yard fanatic. Always out front between two and three-thirty in the afternoons. An ordinary man in his late fifties with a big jowly face, heavy-beard but close-shaved, thinning black (dyed) hair pasted over his scalp. Short spindly legs supporting a thick torso. Skinny legs sticking out of scotch-plaid Bermuda shorts while he weed-whacked his sidewalk edges.

Good, I thought; he must pay. I kept him in sight until he returned inside his house. I learned he was a creature of habit, like me. He rewarded himself after these midday labors. During my second week of surveillance, I was approaching the same cracked sidewalk panel when he roared off to the VFW for a few hours of drinking. He always returned between six-thirty and eight. No wife or kids apparently. Divorced or widower, I didn't know or care. Not a visitor in the entire time I watched from a distance.

It was time to act. I was all set for the next afternoon. I had everything I needed packed and stored in a U-Haul rental trailer. I had custom-made business logos designed from a kit ready to be applied to the sides of the trailer.

I tend to overdo, so I had to fight my impulse to prolong surveillance. I rarely left home since formulating my plan, but this night was an exception. I needed to think it all through as I walked, assessing and anticipating every possible contingency as if it were a bank heist. By the time I returned home at dawn for a few hours of sleep, I was ready.

I drank my morning coffee and watched the sun come up, first painting the world in soft pastels, dappling rooftops and then trees. For the first time in years, I felt my body respond to the world's turning as it matched the rhythm of nature's rise and fall of sap. Full daylight was just moments away.

I didn't hate Sinatra Man in those few moments of peace.

I pulled into his driveway with my trailer fifteen minutes after he left for his VFW session. Once he'd left and come back a minute later for something he'd forgotten so I had to be alert.

Stepping out of my rental car, a nondescript

Toyota, I tugged my khaki shirt into my belt, casually looking about for any sign that I had disturbed normalcy—discounting the huge plastic gray Halloween rat affixed to the top of the trailer to complement the fake business decals pasted up.

He had one of those cheap doors Lowe's sells for a hundred bucks. I'd practiced on one at home for hours with a lockpick and instructions from the internet. If it didn't open, I intended to use a beveled wedge and ram it with my shoulder, even though that might draw some heads peeking through sheers across the street. Every neighborhood, I discovered, has at least one insomniac, a gossip, and a spy. My hands shook badly. I focused, zeroed out my mind and breathed; it clicked and the door opened with a soft pop.

I stood there listening for a long moment. Then I headed for the Sinatra Room. I didn't need to do this, and I shouldn't have, but I needed to see it whole from the inside. The light switch showed it to be every bit as tacky as those nighttime images revealed from my camera.

I worked fast inside but controlled myself

outside—no hectic movements and a few showy displays of my "exterminator man" props were enough to allay anyone's curiosity, I hoped. Once inside with the boxes of material arranged in a precise order, I went to work. For every poster I took down, a new one went up. For every Sinatra item removed from a shelf, one replaced it as close to its genus as I could effect—even the mannequin was situated in the identical spot at the correct angle. When I had all his artifacts placed in my boxes, I saw my measurements were an exact fit and counterbalance. Yin and yang. I gave myself a silent kudo for getting it right. The last items were the stack of CDs I brought to replace the Sinatra ones. Just as in the universe, matter has an edge over antimatter, so too I was deficient in the number of CDs and of course no vinyl records existed to replace his. I therefore compensated with extra CD copies.

I was in the house for exactly one hour and nineteen minutes—two minutes longer than my best practice effort but still good. I shut off the light and closed the door three-quarters as he had left it.

The last part was also going to risk exposure

but here, too, I had some cover in the big steel canister with its spray nozzle. The folding stepladder in my other hand wouldn't attract curiosity. Anyone looking would assume I was working as an exterminator. Once I was safely obscured in the back of the house, I took out the wireless high-resolution minicamera I'd bought from Amazon for forty-five bucks that sent the digital signals to my laptop and included audio. I used the stepladder to position the camera on the far ledge. Sinatra Man would see it sooner or later, but I was interested in first reactions, not a long-term relationship.

Back home, I set up my computer to record everything to the disk in the hard drive. I was desperate to sit at the screen, but there was work to be done first. I emptied the trailer's contents into my shed. I uncoupled the trailer and drove it back to the U-Haul place. I called a taxi to take me back home. The rental car was returned and a different taxi picked me up for the return trip.

He arrived home two hours after I'd left. Sinatra Man's reaction was everything I had hoped it would be. He didn't check the room until ten that night but it was worth the wait. Once the ceiling light blazed on, he did a crazy stutter-step backwards like a man stumbling over a ledge. Then he fell to his knees and howled. It made me shiver, I tell you. He didn't say much—that is, if you discount the repetitious curses and innumerable 'Oh my Gods.'

He attacked the room. He ripped every Ramones poster off the wall. I watched Joey, Johnny, Dee Dee, and Tommy get mashed up and tossed. He raved while he tore the limbs off that expensive lanky mannequin of Joey. He smashed Joey's head against the wall. In minutes, the whole room was trashed and everything, including the CDs, was lying on the floor: glass-framed concert tickets, signed memorabilia, shot glasses, Ramones t-shirts, wrist bands, handbills, even a rare Marky Ramones signed Punk Rock Blitzkrieg. What with all the scams out there with autographs signed by secretaries, I knew I was being upright in getting authentic material. It didn't matter; he even stomped on the pile and kicked some of it out the doorway.

Sinatra Man never called the police. I admired him for that. After a few minutes, exhausted and done weeping and swearing, he left the room and I could no longer hear him. About two in the morning, he returned; he stood calmly in the doorway. A strange look on his face, not of wrath as before or hurt as later, but a new look. He was transfixed by the spectacle.

I could have wept. I knew then: we were cuffed together in this universe. Maybe, too, deep in his neocortex or perhaps deeper in his paleocortex where habits are created and stored like the regrets that pile up around us like unread books, he knew me. Knew my essence, my existence somewhere in this strange world we now shared. I showed him normal things were a lie, a joke. Things he could now comprehend because we were brothers in solidarity and sorrow.

I do plan to return his stuff one day. Meanwhile I'm just biding my time.

Pay for Do

Michael W. Clark

Patrolman Jake Clifton was chopping wood on the side of the road. Instead of sitting in his cruiser, wasting gas keeping the heat going and just sitting there getting fat and out of shape, he chopped wood. He generated his own heat and wasn't bored. Anyway, up this high, he could spot any reckless vehicle, long before they zoomed past him.

Mostly, violations up here were drug transport issues. Violators reacted in strange ways. Most just gave up but some made life extra interesting. Jake liked being a state policeman, out here in the forests. There was just too much city in the city – too many people. Out here there were fewer, far fewer and that was the way he liked it. Those few violators who didn't immediately give up tended to be more violent than most, but Jake liked that too. He would never say this to anyone, but he did like it. He liked it like he liked chopping wood. The air was cold but he wasn't. He smiled a lot on this job.

The noise of a mammoth engine made him smile too. Something was about to happen. He wiped his axe with an old beach towel and placed it in the trunk. The truck was roaring louder, getting closer. He put on his hat and jacket. He thought about picking up the shot gun, but that would start everyone on a bad foot. Shot guns generated attitudes, mostly negative ones. He left the trunk open instead. He turned to the outlet of the old mountain path. It opened up onto the highway right at this bend. It was the reason he chopped wood here. The truck was coming up the path but before the truck came out of the trees a naked man ran out.

'Too cold for naked!' Jake shouted at the man.

The man screamed at seeing Jake and ran off at an angle along the highway.

'Hey? Where are your clothes?' Jake yelled, but the truck noise was too great.

A 4x4 banged over the tree roots. Its tires dug at the earth, struggling to climb over the natural obstructions. Technology triumphed and the 4x4 jumped up onto highway.

Jake yelled at the 4x4 but couldn't even hear his own voice. The 4x4 paid less attention to Jake than the naked man did and raced down the highway in the same direction as the naked man. Jake watched as the vehicle screeched to a halt, its engine died as its driver jumped out and ran into the trees close to where the naked man had entered.

'At least, he has clothes on,' Jake muttered as he slammed the trunk down. Jake checked that the snap cover on his holster was secure and then he ran after the two men. They hadn't broken any laws yet, other than maybe needing a permit for off road driving. There wasn't a law against running naked in the forest. It wasn't a smart thing to do, but as long as he wasn't in a public gathering area, who would know? It did look like laws were about to be broken though. Jake should follow, he would call it in when he found out what it was.

As he ran down the highway his mobile rang his mother's song. She had written it for herself and loaded it on his phone. She wrote a theme song for him to encourage him when the day got long and disappointing. He loved his mother but he didn't like her music. He never told her that. He picked up as he walked fast across the highway. 'In pursuit Mom. This important?' He tried to use as cheery a tone as he could. Apparently, it wasn't cheery enough.

'You like your criminals better than your mother.'

'Not true Mom. I do like my job though.' He looked down into the wood were they ran - no path. It would make for slower going, especially if you're naked. 'Is it life or death?'

'Everything is, in a way.'

'You take too many pills again?' Jake jogged into the trees pushing through the brush. He could hear the men up ahead.

'Not too many.' She sighed. 'Just enough to want the best of life for you. My only son.'

'Ok. Ok.' Jake stopped moving. 'Mom, go for a walk. I'll call later.'

'Off to your criminals then.' She hung up.

'Later Mater.' Jake smiled. He could just see the two men in a small clearing created by a tree fall. Jake moved forward quietly and listened. Maybe this was a romance thing.

'You pale spawn!' one man barked.

'What does that mean?' the other man asked.

'It's just an insult.'

'If I don't understand it, how can I be insulted?'

Jake nodded in agreement. He didn't comprehend half of the things perps yelled at him, so the perp's effort was wasted. Significance of tone isn't enough. All perps were pissed off at him, that never hurt his feelings either. It made him laugh, mostly.

'Well, I was being spontaneous.'

'You shouldn't! You need to practice your insults.'

'That is the opposite of spontaneous.'

Jake nodded in agreement again. When Jake was close enough he could see the naked man was on his knees with the 4x4 guy standing behind him grabbing his hair. A sex thing, Jake thought. He looked behind and saw that they weren't visible from the highway. Again, as long as there was no public intrusion… Jake started to turn back then came the loud smack.

'No need for me to practice that!' The 4x4 guy yelled. 'Understand that?'

The naked guy was on the ground.

'He might not understand, but I'm beginning to." Jake muttered as he turned back toward the couple. No one liked domestic disputes. Jake walked up to the edge of the clearing. 'You guys! Hey! You guys?'

The 4x4 guy had pulled the naked guy up. They both looked over at Jake. The naked guy repeated his previous response to Jake and screamed. The sound made the 4x4 guy jump back in surprise, he let go of the naked guy's hair and the naked guy fell back on to the ground. At least he stopped screaming, but started crying.

'Look! Like the song says, You shouldn't beat the one you love.' Jake pointed at the naked guy.

'He's not my lover!'

'Ok, breaking up is hard to do, but no breakage need occur.' Jake smiled. With domestic disputes, Jake thought a positive mood was best to control such situations. Threats begot threats.

'God! I'm not gay.' Shouted the 4x4 guy.

'Alternative life style. No need for derogatory terms.' Jake tried a firm but pleasant tone.

'Christ!' The 4x4 guy shouted reaching into his jacket.

Jake unholstered his gun and aimed at the 4x4 guy before his hand was visible again. 'Carefully!' Jake raised his voice into command tone. 'We were just talking. No offense meant.' Jake watched every motion in detail.

'Wait! Wait! Just a paper.' The 4x4 guy's tone changed too. 'It's a contract.' He threw the paper onto the ground.

'Noooo!' Shouted the naked guy as he grabbed at the paper.

Jake stomped his boot down on the paper just as the naked guy got his hand on it. The naked guy screamed louder and pulled his hand back. This action caused Jake to slip off balance and fall to his right side.

'I'm not going to jail for you!' The 4x4 guy shouted kicking at the still scrambling naked guy. He crabbed backwards with the contract in his hand.

'Show him the contract!'

"No! It has my name on it.' The naked guy crawled into a bush.

'It's got my name on it too, asshole!' The 4x4 guy kicked at the bush the naked guy hid in.

'Both of you stop!' Jake had gotten to his feet. He kicked the 4x4 guy behind the knee causing him to fall backwards with his right leg bent underneath him. Jake stepped on the 4x4 guy's right shoulder. "Stop before you get hurt."

'I'm hurt now.'

'Ok. Hurt more.' Jake smiled down at him. 'Calm the fuck down! Both of you.' The naked guy cried, stood up and started to run. Jake sighed pulled out his taser and fired. The naked guy fell forward mid-stride as the voltage went through his body. 'Told you to stop, damn it!' Jake took out his cuffs, attached one to the wrist of the 4x4 guy. 'Get up and come over here.' Jake pulled him up and walked over to the quivering body of the naked guy. Jake attached the other cuff to the left wrist of the naked guy.

'I could get electrocuted too! Don't.' The 4x4 guy pulled back.

'Nahhh! There is just one jolt at the beginning.' Jake jerked out the electrodes. They left two small bloody puncture wounds. 'Sit him up.'

The 4x4 guy pulled the quivering guy up. 'Oh, Christ! He's got a hard on.'

'Electricity can be exciting. What are you complaining about? You were chasing a naked guy. What did you expect to happen?' Jake rolled his eyes shaking his head.

'I was paid to just chase and abuse. No sex stuff.'

Jake laughed. 'Sounds a bit like my job description.' Jake broke off a low branch from a Maple tree growing at the edge of the clearing. 'Use this to cover Adam here.' He threw it at the 4x4 guy. 'Where's that contract?' Jake scanned the clearing. It was where the naked guy fell.

Jake started laughing as he read the pages. 'Guess his significant other isn't game. Ha!'

'He signed it,' the 4x4 guy pointed.

Jake laughed. 'How do I know Adam's real name? He doesn't have ID on him.' Jake forced himself not to laugh again.

'His stuff is all back there with his car.'

Jake broke out laughing again. 'Slap Adam awake here and let's verify that. Remember to hold up the branch if he can't. We don't want the public to see this.'

'Christ, no!' The 4x4 guy pulled Adam to a standing position. He was crying.

'He always this emotional?' Jake rolled his eyes.

The 4x4 guy shrugged. 'Don't know. First time I ever met the guy.'

At Adam's car, he got into his clothes as Jake typed his driver's license number into the cruiser keyboard. The names matched. 'You're a doctor?' Jake shouted out the cruiser's open passenger door. Adam nodded as he buttoned his shirt.

'Not a psychiatrist, I hope?' Jake smiled.

Dr. Adam didn't say anything.

'Oh shit.' The 4x4 guy muttered standing beside him.

'Oh shit indeed.' Jake laughed, then 'Sorry. Sorry, sir, who am I to judge?'

'You're a cop.' Dr. Adam said.

'Yeah, yeah, I am at that,' Jake chuckled. 'Wait till my mom hears about this.'

'So you're arresting me?' Dr. Adam pulled on his down vest.

Jake frowned and smiled at the same time. 'For what? You're not illegally distributing drugs or something?'

'I'm certainly not,' the 4x4 guy chipped in.

Dr. Adam also shook his head. 'So I can go?'

'If you feel like it,' Jake shrugged. 'I would keep my abuse and humiliation events more private from now on. Is my advice.'

'Can I go too?'

"Sure. I'm not stopping you.' Jake reached across to close the passenger door.

The 4x4 ran over. 'Can you give me a ride back to my truck?'

'No,' Jake shook his head. 'They don't pay me to be a taxi and I've got to call my mother.' Jake laughed pulling the door closed. He would call her after he stopped laughing. 'I love this job,' Jake said to himself. 'Better than chopping wood.'

Dumping Ground

David Rachels

I've found nine skulls so far, and I'm not sure if I should keep looking. I'm fairly deep in the woods, at least half a mile from the highway, but if I hang around too long, there's always the chance that someone will catch me here. I must say, though, the fact that nobody's found any of these bones yet must mean that I'm fairly safe.

I wish I had kept things more organized around here, laid the bodies in rows or something, but it was chaos at the start. I dumped that first body as fast as I could and ran. When I made it home, I couldn't believe the police weren't following me. I dumped the second body somewhere close by just because I hadn't got caught here first time. That was pretty much the story with body number three as well.

Over time, I started to calm down, sort of a like a teenager when he starts having sex. Body number one had been like a premature ejaculation, but by number five or six, I had things under control.

I made the mistake, however, of not getting organized. I started taking my time with each dump, savoring each one, but I still wasn't paying attention to the bigger picture, and now I'm looking at a mess.

How many bodies are here? That's what I want to know. I've kept no trophies, written no diary. I've thought about making some tick marks somewhere, but even that seems too risky. I want nothing in my apartment (or in a storage locker or anywhere else) that might incriminate me. I'm smart about stuff like this, even when I come here. Case in point, I always masturbate when I'm here, but I always wear condom. I'm sophisticated that way.

The media are starting to suspect there's a serial killer on the loose, but their count is no good. They've tied together only four of my killings so far, and it's driving me crazy that I don't know if I've found those four particular skulls yet. I wish there was some other bone I could count, but skulls are the only ones I recognize. Of course, I might have found them all by now if it wasn't for the fact that skulls are the most fun bone to play with, even if they do have a tendency to tear holes in condoms, and when I'm done using them I have a tendency to toss them aside. How far do I toss them? Where do they land? It's enough to make me give up.

I've think I've been here for about two hours, and I haven't found a skull for at least twenty minutes, so maybe it's time to go. Nine kills is about the number I remember, so maybe I have my answer. I have the skulls lined up in a row at my feet and I'm tearing open a condom when I happen to look heavenward for the first time. I'm trying to use the sun to judge the time of day, but I can't see much of the sky through all the trees. Then I start looking around at the branches, and it isn't long before I spot a skull hanging in a tree with a branch through one eye socket.

All right then, I'll call it ten, but now I have to get that last skull down. I go to shimmy up the tree, but before I latch myself to the trunk, I pause to finish putting on the condom. Like I told you, I'm sophisticated that way.

Backlit

Nell Pates

There is a face print on the glass. An ugly, grey smear, greasy where his nose and cheeks butted up on the pane. You can make out the wide, raw shape of the mouth if you look closely.

There is a face print on the window of this pretty, secluded cottage with its delicate rose creeping up a trellis by the front door. The face stands out between two bold smudges that show where he beat the glass with his hands and then his fists.

Frail old man. He beat it and beat it and beat it. He hollered and screamed and then he howled.

He was looking at me - hopeful, I think, at first - but he fell back eventually. He fell back when he finally understood.

Earlier, when I let myself in, quietly, through the back door (a spare key left under a conspicuous solitary flower pot!) I took a moment to look about me: the single plate, knife and fork drying by the sink, a stack of *Reader's Digest* magazines by the couch forming an orderly mountain of mundanity, plain photographs in plain frames above the electric fire. These last spoke of a dull life, lived carefully.

There was one of the old man as a young man, holding hands with a girl in long skirts beneath a tall tree in some bland patch of countryside that could have been anywhere, then a standard, boring wedding portrait of the same pair, half-smiling. A picture of the old man sitting in some outside space next to the old woman that the young girl must have become with the onward march of time.

He was on his own now.

There was nothing special about this old man's life - nothing to recommend it. His collection of old *Reader's Digest* back-issues was probably the best thing he had been able to build in his life, but for its expanse it was nonetheless average. Every elderly person in the country seemed to maintain a blossoming stack of that old tripe.

There were no children - I checked. I would not want you waste any time in mourning for him. No one else will.

I opened all the doors downstairs, quiet and

slow, then locked the front door and all the windows. I put the keys in a random kitchen drawer on my way to the gas hob.

This I lit - all four rings - and then I picked half the stack of magazines from the pile and offered them to the flames. As they caught I added tea towels, and left another pile of magazines in easy reach of the blaze - in a good position to convey the fire to the kitchen curtains.

Having finished, I slipped out of the back door - locking it behind me and replacing the key beneath the flower pot - then I headed round to the front garden.

I thought at first that he must have caught the smoke and died that way, because nothing happened for a while, but all of a sudden the lights were on in the bedroom, the hallway, and there was a really desperate sort of rattling at the front door.

No key.

That was when he moved to the living room - a surprising amount of fight from the old man. I saw him, backlit, as he fumbled at the edge of the curtains looking for the key he'd hung so carefully on a little golden string. Almost certainly hung in case of fire. He didn't find it - how could he? - so he moved to hit the glass.

Impressive stuff double glazing.

At first I think he was just trying to break out, but that was before he saw me. That was when he pushed his big old head right up to the glass.

I don't know how long it took for him to realise that I wasn't motionless through shock or fear. I was watching.

No help to be forthcoming, I'm afraid.

I liked watching his face as he realised. It was after it dawned on him that he started up his howling. The howling came before the coughing and before he fell down.

Now the whole place is dancing with flames, the garden alive with flickering, shape-shifting shadows in the gloom, and all that's left is the face on the glass.

I break that pane with a rock, and step back as fresh oxygen breathes life afresh into the furnace. A small piece of evidence, this sign of distress, but nevertheless it is worth disposing of it.

I'll call the fire services and let them know I broke a window to try and help but it was no good. I'll be terribly distressed on the phone - won't leave my name, and I'll hang up quickly. The phone will be in the canal within an hour. I'll be gone long before anyone gets here.

It's not like it's my first time.

Step one: identify the target. It should be someone that nobody will miss - homeless, drop-out, widowed, childless - any loser or loner will do.

Step two: conceive such a method of expunging the sad little candle of life from the pathetic vessel in which it resides that with a little shortsightedness it might be thought an accident or a suicide.

Step three: lather. Rinse. Repeat.

The trick - the *art* - is in this repetition. The pattern must be to set no pattern. Do not just target old ladies in their homes. Do not only pick up homeless nobodies from the streets, never to return them. Do not use only fire, or gas, poison or a 'fall'.

Do not steal - or, if you must, steal randomly rather than trophy hunting.

Organised randomness.Ritual chaos.

By thinking, by planning, by following the steps: I succeed.

The truth is this: You are far, far more likely to be dispatched through foul play by a person known to you - a lover, relative or friend. There will be a motive to uncover, blame to be apportioned, and motive found followed by blame served are the diligent forerunners of justice done.

And yet, whispers the voice at the back of your mind, and *yet*, there are still those of us who will kill you for the pure joy of the thing.

Unrivalled it its simplicity.

We will find you, if you are vulnerable to our rules, then we will find a way.

There are killers, those who do not follow my methods, who kill for sport or for trophies. Such sport hunters are easily hunted and captured. They do not follow my process.

Take the case of a fire in an old man's house, with no family to squawk and wail - if an investigation is even done it will be lacklustre and half-hearted at best: conducted by officials with no press on their backs and no interest in the outcome. It will burn out as quickly as these amber flames.

Murder? Accident? Suicide?

Who knows, who cares? Let's grab a doughnut!

And the next time?

And the next.

And the next.

I will be there, but I will not be seen through my orchestrated chaos.

Because the truth that matters is this: I am going to kill you.

I am going to kill you for no other purpose than to watch you die.

Slaughterhouse Girls

Kurt Newton

Born the daughters of butcher men,
they played amid the death-throe sounds,
with pigskin dollies and cow bone tea sets,
and dress-up jewelry made from teeth.

As teens the girls held late night rendezvous
with boys inside the empty stalls,
but their tendencies towards hooks and chains
kept many a would be suitor home.

But every now and then they'd find a boy
who didn't mind a fumble in the dark,
dressed in rubber boots, apron and little else,
standing ankle-deep in blood.

The girls have all grown up now,
some came close but never married.
After a series of unfortunate accidents
they took over the family business.

Now the men who line up to enter their lives
are either pigs or stubborn bulls.
The girls didn't outgrow their tendencies,
now it's the knives that fascinate them most.

Nursing Home Boys

Kurt Newton

The product of late night tussles
with Viagra-stoked octogenarians;
birthed from dry-gulch wombs
that had lain dormant for fifty years.

More wrinkled than your average newborn,
like a Sharpei with opposable thumbs;
kept hidden in laundry rooms and linen closets
by a dozen doting grandmothers.

But despite their ninety pound heroic measures,
only the boys would tend to survive,
nursing on skin-flaked nipples daubed with pabulum
beneath the scent of bed sore salve.

They've grown up now to be the janitors
who work the lonely late night shift;
toothless, hairless, and nearly sightless,
they still find time to nurse.

He Wouldn't Snitch

Leroy B. Vaughn

Elmo Parker watched the streets as he and Bumper Morgan cruised down Carson Street. It was early November and it was starting to cool off fast outside.

It would be dark in another hour and Bumper had already taken his tuffy jacket out of the trunk of the patrol car. Elmo turned on his transistor radio and played along with Danny and the Juniors with his night stick, pounding out the rhythm on the dashboard of the patrol car.

'Good thing cars don't have metal dashboards anymore,' Bumper told him as he grinned at his partner.

Elmo and Bumper were street cops in Las Vegas, Nevada. Their beat was in the downtown district. It was the 1970s and Vegas was not the trendy nightclub/disco scene or giant adult Disneyland that people see on television today. Their part of Vegas was the rundown section of downtown that included Las Vegas Blvd., north of the famous Vegas strip. They didn't see all the cool rat pack dudes with the chicks in the cocktail dresses, going over to the Dunes to drop a few bucks at the craps table or on the roulette wheel. Theirs was the honky tonk, rundown, beat up, down-on-your-luck part of Vegas with the flop house hotels, wedding chapels with Elvis impersonators, massage parlors, cheap hotels that rented by the week or month, tattoo parlors, dive bars and liquor stores.

'Friday night in the city,' Elmo said as Bumper rounded the corner and headed towards Bridger St. 'We gonna see some ambulance riding tonight,' he told Bumper.

Elmo was a veteran of six years with the Detroit Police Department and Bumper had about the same amount of time with the Vegas P.D. These were the days of the old blue police uniforms. Vegas was starting to become a good sized city and it had all the crime of the bigger cities over in California. The cops all knew that a lot of the crime came from California and other states. Vegas was one of those places no one was born in. Bumper Morgan had lived in Vegas since the early fifties, when his parents had moved there after the war. He was almost a native by Nevada standards.

Elmo Parker was glad to be out of the cold weather and urban decay of Detroit. For him, the rundown part of Vegas was a nice place to work after spending all that time in a patrol car in Detroit.

They drove past Bob Stupak's Fabulous Vegas World and Bumper asked Elmo if he wanted a hot dog. 'I think I'll wait a while and catch a bowl of chili beans, if we don't get too busy tonight,' Elmo explained as he lit an Old Gold cigarette. Bumper didn't mind the smoke in the car too much. Both cops always left their windows open, except the rare times that it rained.

Bumper pulled into the red zone at Vegas World and started to get out, leaving the engine running, when the call came in. 'Man down, possible shots fired,' the dispatcher said as Bumper threw the shifter into gear while Elmo hit the lights and siren. Cars pulled to the side as Bumper told Elmo, 'Ah, their playing my song,' listening to the siren scream.

Three minutes earlier, De'John Jackson had walked out of the Apache Motel, all pimped out in his long purple coat, lime green slacks, oversize white super fly pimp daddy hat and gold colored platform shoes. De'John was headed to the dive bar down the street to line his bitch up for the night. He was going to have to slap her around a little if she didn't turn more tricks tonight. A man had to have some money in a town like Las Vegas.

De'John had the pimp walk down and was strutting his stuff as he bounced his walking stick on the side walk. He hadn't been paying much attention, and then he looked up and saw Tyrone Mimms coming at him.

Tyrone was one bad ass mofo and he had warned De'John to stay off of Las Vegas Blvd. He had looked into De'Johns eyes and said, 'I thought I told you to get your punk ass out of town niggah.'

De'John wasn't going to waste any time with this jive ass turkey. De'John went for the straight razor that was in his coat pocket, but it was too late. Before he could pull the razor, Tyrone already had his thirty two gun, the same caliber that Bad Bad Leroy Brown carried just for fun, out of his pocket and aimed it at De'John.

Tyrone pulled the trigger three times and De'John went down. At least eight people were on the street, or sitting on the porch of the flop house, but there would not be anyone to tell the cops what happened when they arrived on the scene.

Bumper slammed the patrol car to a stop in front of the man that was lying on the sidewalk. Elmo bailed out and was tearing the man's shirt open, while Bumper went to the trunk of the car to get the first aid kit. Dispatch had called for an ambulance after Bumper and Elmo got the call and they could both hear the ambulance siren in the distance. Elmo pressed on the man's chest and there was blood all over his hands as Morgan made mental notes of the scene.

Both cops had seen the punk before, but didn't know his name. Bumper saw the straight razor on the ground and the walking stick on the other side of the man.

He looked at the man's right hand and saw that

he was holding a twenty-dollar bill. Elmo gave Bumper the look that said, this dude is not going to make it, and Bumper pulled a note book from his back pocket.

The ambulance had arrived and the medics started to load the man into the ambulance. Bumper told Elmo that he would ride with the ambulance and try to get a dying declaration from the man, while Elmo followed them to the hospital in the patrol car. The man did not look good and the medic told Bumper that he was not going to make it to the hospital. The odd thing was that the man was still holding onto the twenty dollar bill.

Bumper got real close to the man's face and said. 'You're going to die. Tell me who shot you, so we can take him to jail.'

'I ain't telling you shit pig.' The man said as he gasped for air. The chest wound was making a sucking sound and the medic was getting ready to place the oxygen mask over his mouth to help him breathe.

Bumper asked him again to tell him the name of the man that would soon be a killer. 'I ain't no snitch man. The brother gave me twenty bucks and told me not to say shit.'

Bumper looked at the man as he died and removed the twenty dollar bill from his hand.

A Spontaneous Decision

Kathleen A. Ryan

A wave of regret washed over Erin's body. She curses her spontaneous decision to leave the front door not only unlocked, but ajar; all to appease her husband, Sam, after their nearly marriage-ending argument the night before. He bitched yet again over having to use a key to enter their four-bedroom colonial when Erin was already inside. She reiterated the justification of her cop rules, and even reminded him of his firefighter's precautions that he insists upon and how she doesn't mind.

Tonight, in order to make nice, Erin begins cooking Sam's favorite dinner of chicken cutlets, mashed potatoes and corn. She sets the dining room table, where they rarely eat their meals nowadays, and lights fragrant pine-scented candles on this chilly winter evening to set the mood.

During her day tour, Erin arranged with her sister to keep Sophie overnight, so she and Sam could spend a romantic evening together.

New York-style cheesecake and uninterrupted make-up sex to be included, of course.

She hesitates briefly to break one of her diehard rules, or 'obsessions' as Sam prefers to call them, and leaves the front door ajar.

The creepy sound of the front door creaking open at a snail's pace, sans the sound of Sam whooping it up, gets her adrenalin going. Although pissed at her own actions, she is at least grateful that she had just turned off the 5 o'clock news in order to hear Sam's entrance.

Instead, an uncomfortable silence fills the air. Her suspicions rise and her pulse quickens.

At this particular moment, it's imperative to toss the anger and act quickly.

She edges closer to the hallway which leads to the front door.

An imposing intruder, armed with a glistening, serrated knife, emerges. Tactical options flood her mind while evaluating the situation.

In a deep, raspy voice, the stranger whispers, "Even I lock my door when I'm home alone."

Fleetingly, she contemplates the irony of the

situation as this monster admonishes her — the Queen Door Locker — but the severity of the situation sinks in. Before she can form a response, Sam strides in — rejoicing over a keyless entry.

The startled stranger swings behind Erin, pressing the blade against her neck. Stunned, Sam freezes. As the stranger barks orders at Sam, a fire alarm goes off as the smell of burning food fills the air and it startles the burglar. Erin swiftly lifts up the heel of her foot, rips the Glock from her ankle holster, shoves it into the belly of the beast and fires away.

The stranger crumples to the floor.

Color returns to Sam's pale face. As he rushes to retrieve a fire extinguisher, he turns around and admits, 'You know, honey, of all your — um, precautions, the gun in the ankle is my absolute favorite.'

Down the Devil Hole

J. David Jaggers

Baby Jesse was an unexpected but welcome addition to the Johnson household. She arrived during a time of relative prosperity, a time before Abe Johnson turned mean and stayed buried in the bottom of a corn whiskey jar. Abe had a steady job down at the mill, and made enough money to keep his wife and eight year old son Flint fed and sheltered. The new baby girl was greeted as a blessing, a sign of good things to come. Flint didn't really know how to feel about his new little sister. He was curious when they brought her home, but she cried a lot and his momma was so busy taking care of her that he felt invisible. After a month or so, the baby calmed down and seeing that there wasn't much space in the tiny house, Abe put her crib in Flint's room. Flint would lay awake at night just to listen to her coo and chirp like babies do.

That fall, when the holler's green started turning to rusty orange, Flint's daddy brought home that damned doll. He had seen it down at the Five and Dime in Bronson and thought little Jesse would like it. It was a miniature baby, made of cloth with a blue dress and a pale ceramic face carved into a smile. For some reason that little doll scared the hell out of Flint. When the moon was out, the light would shine in the little window above his bed and he could see that frozen face, lit up like a ghost in the darkness, staring glassy eyed at him through the bars of the crib. It wasn't long after that it started talking to him.

It was a whisper at first, just when he was on the edge of sleep. He'd hear a tiny voice, thin like the tinkling of a bell. He couldn't make out the words, but he was sure it was coming from that doll. He asked his daddy to get rid of it, but Abe just laughed and said he'd bust Flint's ass if he kept whining like a little queer boy. After that it got louder. The voice grew until the words were as clear as day and Flint had to strain to focus on anything else.

That doll was telling him to smother the baby.

By mid-October, when the frost was starting to stick to the pumpkins in the little patch behind the house, Flint felt something in his mind come loose.

He'd been fighting hard to ignore the voice, but he was getting tired and one night he woke up standing over the crib with his pillow in his hands. Little Jesse was sound asleep and looked like an angel laying there in the dim light. The doll was in the corner of the crib, smiling and silent. He'd managed to stop himself then, but he knew he couldn't hold out forever.

One morning, Flint was having a dream. He was standing in the middle of a dirt road in his underwear and a six point buck came crashing through the trees. It stopped right in front of him, snorting steam in the freezing air. Its throat was cut and blood ran down the animal's chest in thick rivulets making the ground muddy at its feet. Flint woke up to his momma screaming.

Baby Jesse was dead.

The doctor from town said it was something called crib death, but Flint knew better. The voice in his head was gone, and his hands hurt like he'd squeezed something real hard. He wanted to tell his daddy that it was him who'd smothered little Jesse, but by then Abe had fallen apart, spending the next two weeks out in the little shed behind the house, drunk on corn whiskey. Flint could hear him at all hours of the night, cursing and weeping. Flint's momma tried to help, but Abe was inconsolable. When he finally did come out, he looked like a wild man, his hair and beard tangled in knots. He stormed into the house and grabbed up the crib and everything in it, and dragged it back through the woods to the old sink hole that Flint called the devil hole, where they dumped the garbage.

The death of baby Jesse marked the end of life as Flint knew it. From then on things got bleak. Abe lost his job at the mill on account of showing up drunk, and when Flint's momma dared say something about it, he'd beat her until she couldn't move for days. Flint stayed hid up in the woods when it got that bad. He learned early on to stay out of his old man's way. He had a small fort built from dead tree limbs up the deer path on the ridge overlooking the property. He and the neighbor boy down the road, Eugene Pritchard would sit up there sometimes and Flint would listen to Eugene talk about life outside the holler.

'I'm gonna move down to Boiling Springs when I get old enough,' Eugene would say. 'My uncle Jimmy said they always need laborers down there cause of the college.' Flint couldn't get his head around the idea of college. Who would volunteer for more school?

About the time the boys entered fifth grade, Flint started hearing the voice again, but only when he walked out to the sink hole to throw out the week's garbage. His daddy was broke down and on disability and stayed so drunk he couldn't lift a finger most of the time. Flint did all the chores to help out his momma, but he dreaded every time he had to go back to that hole, dragging the trash bag behind him down the trail. When the voice started getting louder, he'd sometimes catch himself standing at the edge, just staring down into the darkness, looking for the face of that doll.

'Leave me alone!' he would scream, but nothing ever answered.

Flint couldn't remember when he started killing small animals and throwing them down the devil hole, it had become a ritual. It seemed to him that he had always done it, but some part of him knew that wasn't right. He started with squirrels and rabbits, using his rusty pen knife to slit their throats before chucking them into the blackness. It was like he was feeding something, something terrible that lived down there.

The day that six point buck jumped out of the tree line when Flint and Eugene were walking down the dirt road was a turning point. From that moment on, the hole demanded bigger offerings. Some hunter had shot the deer, but missed the mark and its guts were hanging out and dragging the ground behind it. The voice in Flint's head had been screaming at him for days to feed the hole and without thinking he pulled his pen knife and cut that buck's throat right in front of Eugene; it made him feel powerful.

It was all Flint could do to resist the urge to stop and drag the carcass back right then, but he knew Eugene would think badly of him so he managed to hold on until the end of the day. After Eugene had gone on home for supper, Flint snuck out and pulled the carcass back down the road to his house. He struggled with the heavy beast, but after an hour he had it tipped at the edge of the hole, his foot on its bloated belly.

The gaping pit had always smelled bad, as far back as Flint could remember, but since he started feeding it, a dark odor began to rise up. He had lost count of all the creatures he had bled out and dumped down there. The voice was still the same, a steady thrum, always urging him to feed the blackness. Flint used his toe to push the stiff deer over the edge, the dirty entrails slid along the edge for a second after the body disappeared.

After Flint's daddy died from cancer, they buried him at the back corner of the property under a dogwood tree that he had liked. As the men from the funeral home lowered the casket into the clay, Flint didn't grieve. All he could think about was the devil hole, and how his daddy would've fit in nice down there in the darkness. Eugene came to the funeral. He and Flint were in high school now and Eugene had a car and was a star football player. The boys rode to school together every day and just like when they were kids, Eugene talked about the future while Flint listened.

'Coach says I could get a scholarship if I keep up the hustle and study hard, but I don't know.'

Flint picked his fingernails with the pen knife, and imagined cutting Coach Vincent's throat. He'd yelled at Flint once for falling asleep in class and Flint never forgot it. The thought of his lifeless body slipping down the hole made Flint smile.

Things finally started falling apart when Flint's momma took in a renter to help pay the bills. Abe's disability ended with his death and the bank was about to take the house. The man said his name was Russell and he was a welder down in Bronson. He paid in cash every month and lived out in the shed where Abe used to sit and drink. Russell was a loud talker who told dirty jokes and drank beer. After a while, Flint's momma started taking a liking to him and before long, he'd moved into her room. Flint could hear them going at it through the thin walls every night. Flint began to hate Russell, and the voice grew to a scream, pounded at him every day and every night. He would lie there shaking, listening to the voice compete with the squeak of the mattress and the moans in the next room.

One night after everyone was asleep, he walked out to the hole with his daddy's old flash light. He shined it down into the putrid shadows. There were bones, hundreds of them some white and shiny and some still dull with a film of rotted meat. The hole twisted down into a lower section and Flint moved around the edge to get a better look. He knew it had to be there, somewhere. His heart pounded in his chest and he sucked in his breath when he saw the warped rail of the old crib sticking up from a pile of rotted dog carcasses.

'Leave me alone. You hear me you little bitch?' He screamed down into the inky blackness. 'I ain't gonna do it. You hear me? I ain't gonna kill him.'

There was nothing but silence for an answer. Flint spat in the hole and slung the flashlight. It tumbled down and settled below the crib, lighting up the bottom. Flint screamed and ran back toward the house when he saw half of the doll's ceramic face sticking up, stained brown and a big blue eye staring out at him from a pile of writhing maggots.

No matter what he did, the voice just wouldn't

quit. It had gotten to the point that Flint stopped sleeping all together. He would pace the floors of his room at night, mumbling to himself, oblivious anything going on around him. Finally one morning, he found himself standing out at the edge of the hole at first light. He had his pen knife open in his hand, and he didn't remember how he got there. He heard a voice behind him and turned to see Russell, a blanket wrapped around him and lit cigarette in the corner of his mouth.

'What in the hell are you doin' out here boy?' he said looking at Flint like he had two heads. 'You some kind of sleep walker or somethin'? You walked right past me on the front porch, your eyes as wide as headlights.'

Flint couldn't speak, the voice was thrumming in his head, vibrating every bone in his body. Feed the devil hole. Feed the devil hole. Before he could register what he was doing, he'd closed the distance and had Russell's throat in his grip.

Flint pulled the blade across the man's neck and felt a surge of adrenaline as the hot blood sprayed across his face and pour down his forearm. Russell just stared, bug eyed until the life drained out of him. Flint pushed the limp body toward the hole and watched as Russell slipped over the edge and disappeared into the darkness below. The voice suddenly stopped and for the first time in years, Flint could hear the chirping of the birds and the morning breeze rustling the Sycamore leaves overhead.

The silence didn't last long. By mid-morning the voice had returned, hammering in the back of Flint's skull. He was sitting at the breakfast table listening to his mother pace around, wondering where Russell had taken off to so early. Flint sat quiet and ate his biscuits and gravy, checking his fingernails for any blood he might have missed when he cleaned himself up. A calm had washed over him and he knew he had crossed some kind of line that he couldn't come back from.

Eugene showed up around lunch time and found Flint sitting on the rotten front porch staring out into the distance. 'What the hell you ponderin' about Flint. You gotta awful look on your face.'

Flint grinned, showing his rotten yellow teeth. He pulled out his pocket knife and flipped open the blade. '

     'Hey Eugene, I was just thinkin' about you. Say, you ever seen that old sink hole back at the edge of the property?'

Forget Me Not

Sue Iles-Jonas

You know what it feels like to be really irritated by someone? When even the sound of their breathing makes you clench your fists, never mind the noise they make while eating or turning the pages of the newspaper?

Maureen Potter had more than reached that stage with her husband Frank over the years, but there was now an imperative with his retirement date looming. There was absolutely no way that she could put up with him hanging about the house for the rest of his life when he stopped working.

His 65th birthday was going to fall, as all the other ones had, on 14th February. The rituals of Valentine's Day was something the Potters didn't do. Whereas many people started planning for the day as soon as the Christmas decorations were out of the shop windows Frank had effectively embargoed it when they first met. He'd ruined Valentine's Day every year as she never got anything romantic from him. He'd always said it was his day, and he didn't want it diluted with hearts and flowers nonsense. They never ate out to celebrate, as he refused to get caught up with simpering couples being given poor service by indifferent waiters. 'Besides,' he'd say 'it's cheaper to eat at home.'

Thinking of his retirement she knew that economically divorce was out of the question. She felt that she'd put far too much into this marriage to spend her retirement in reduced circumstances. And indeed why should she?

She considered other options but Maureen had watched enough crime programmes on television to know that modern day forensics made murder too much of a risk for the perpetrator. Frank certainly wasn't worth serving time for, she'd done enough of that by being married to him. It already felt like a life sentence. No, Maureen knew she would need to be more subtly creative.

After a week of close private observation of Frank, as opposed to her usual indifference, Maureen had the outline of a plan.

She took his habits as her baseline and couldn't help but notice that Frank had an unpleasant characteristic that many husbands have. This being selective deafness as far as his wife was concerned. He either didn't hear or pretended not to hear most of what she said first time. He'd raise his head and cock it in an irritating way and say 'sorry dear, what was that?' So she'd have to repeat it, time after time. She'd say to her friends that she thought she might as well have a Dictaphone, record everything she said, and just press the repeat button when he inclined his head in that way that made her want to knock it off its block.

So now, based on her observations, Maureen started speaking much more quietly. She surreptitiously turned down the television and radio, so that Frank began to think that perhaps his hearing wasn't as good as it should be. By the time he went to the doctors for a check-up, she was just about mouthing words, and he had neck ache from craning around trying to pick up sounds. The doctor couldn't find much wrong with Frank in the seven minutes he had with them both. However, as Frank left the room, she hung back and quickly mentioned that she was rather worried about him forgetting things too.

'Oh quite normal at his age, I do it myself,' the doctor said in a cheery but dismissive way. Maureen felt though that she had at least planted the seed of Frank's cognitive impairment in the doctor's mind, even if he didn't note it on Frank's medical record, on this occasion.

Maureen continued her campaign by misplacing Frank's possessions. His teacup would be in different rooms and as for his keys - they seemed to have a life of their own. He was forever saying 'I'm sure they were in my coat pocket......or I know I left them on the hall table.' Maureen would make a big scene about helping to find them 'for him' and they were never where he thought he had left them.

Maureen also took to asking him if he could remember where he had parked the car.

'Of course,' he'd snap, 'it's on the drive, as usual.' But she'd secretly moved it onto the street, and when he looked out of the window to prove his point, he was shocked and worried to see it on the highway. On one occasion when they went to the supermarket she said she'd left the shopping list in the car and went back for it, while Frank got the trolley and made a start on the fruit aisle. While he was choosing the fair trade bananas Maureen deftly moved the car to another section of the car park. When they'd finished their shopping Frank wheeled the trolley out and felt in his pocket for the keys as he made his way to the spot where he knew he'd parked the car.

He paled visibly when he couldn't see it and started running up and down through the bays dragging the trolley erratically as he attempted to locate the vehicle. Maureen feigned horror and surprise that he couldn't remember and walked promptly round the corner to where she'd parked it. Aghast, and shaking his head, he grasped the bags of shopping and put them in the boot with a look of real bewilderment in his eyes. Maureen lost no time talking about his failing memory in hushed tones over coffee with 'the girls', and they in return competed with horror stories of their own husband's aberrations and their lifelong martyrdom.

Frank began to lose confidence, and told people at work that he was getting forgetful, and perhaps it was just as well he was retiring. If he even misplaced a biro, they would say 'Poor old Frank - really losing it now isn't he?'

Maureen cooked extra food, with plenty of fat and sugar and often slipped additional items onto Frank's plate when he wasn't looking. She'd smile and pat his shoulder 'Now eat it all darling, you need to keep your strength up.' He obliged and grew fatter and slower over the months.

She occasionally changed the time on their alarm so he'd oversleep and be late for work. She booked an appointment at the surgery and told the doctor that she was really finding it hard to care for him, but he said that as long as Frank was still working things couldn't be that bad. She'd sigh and pull her shoulders back in that brave way she'd been cultivating of late.

There was no choice then, but to wait for his sixty fifth birthday. Valentine's Day. This year she decided that she would embrace the rituals associated with love. She gave him a cake with a blood red heart and Cupid's arrow shot though the middle, and forget me nots round the edge. She could see in his eyes that he didn't like it, but he'd had a few drinks on his last day at work so he just said 'Thank you' in a gruff voice.

Maureen topped up his glass of wine. 'Good health,' she smiled.

The smoke alarm went off in the early hours started by a tea towel mysteriously left on the hob after Frank had dried the dishes. Maureen insisted that he run to the neighbours for help and in his confusion and slightly drunken state he obeyed without thought. The emergency services accepted Maureen's version of events and what with Frank's unreliable memory, the doctor promptly admitted him for an initial assessment in a residential dementia centre. His protestations were taken as further signs of his compromised cognitive state.

If Maureen hadn't been on the waiting list for a hip replacement she would have skipped around. As it was she could only celebrate with a glass or three of wine and make her way unsteadily, but happily upstairs. Oh, it was so nice not to see the toilet seat left up. It was also good that Frank's dressing gown was missing from the back of the bedroom door.

There was a brief pang of guilt though, when she found a heart shaped box of Valentine's chocolates in her bedroom drawer and Frank's shaky handwriting on a card. 'Sorry I never shared my birthdays with you. Hope this lets you know how I feel.' Love Frank.

Maureen shrugged, 'Too little too late...' Luxuriating in the middle of the empty bed she set to work on the sweets. They were actually very nice truffles by the look of them. Marzipan too, judging from the taste of the first one. You could tell they were handmade as they were a bit heavy on the almonds. Always more taste with handmade. Yes, quite a bitter almond taste, but still lovely. Frank always used to say they used synthetic flavours in cheap chocolates, and he should know, what with being a chemist for all those years.

Bibliographies

Charlie Hughes

Charlie is a 38 year old aspiring writer who has worked in the social and community sectors for most of his life. He writes crime, suspense and horror fiction. Originally from Leeds, He now lives in London. He recently won the Bookers Corner Monthly Writing Competition with his story *The Letter* which will be published in their forthcoming anthology.

Christopher P. Mooney

Christopher P. Mooney (@ChrisPatMooney) was born and brought up in Glasgow and now survives in a small house near London. At various times in his life he has been a supermarket cashier, a shelf stacker, a barman, a cinema usher, a carpet-fitter's labourer and a foreign-language assistant. He is currently a professional teacher of French and English and an amateur writer of crime fiction, horror fiction and eclectic poetry. Since appearing in the inaugural edition of Crooked Holster, his writing has been accepted for publication in print, online and on Kindle by *Spelk Fiction, Dead Guns Press, Devolution Z, Revolution John, Out of the Gutter and YellowMama.*

https://playingwiththepoem.wordpress.com/

David McVey

David McVey lectures in Communication at New College Lanarkshire. He has published over 100 short stories and a great deal of non-fiction that focuses on history and the outdoors. He enjoys hillwalking, visiting historic sites, reading, watching telly, and supporting his home-town football team, Kirkintilloch Rob Roy FC.

David Rachels

David Rachels' short fiction has appeared most recently in *Dark Corners, Shotgun Honey, Near to the Knuckle*, and *Pulp Modern*. His most recent book is an edited collection, *Redheads Die Quickly and Other Stories* by Gil Brewer (UP of Florida, 2012).

Ellis Goodwin

Ellis Goodwin is a writer of prose and poetry often taking a slanted or quirky view of the subjects he takes on. He has had short stories included in two books *Strangers in Paradise* and an online anthology of flash fiction, *Short and Curlies*. He is currently writing a book of indeterminate length and uncertain title.

J. David Jaggers

J. David Jaggers lives in fly-over country, where he spends his days in the white collar world of finance and his nights writing about the degenerates and losers dwelling in shadows of our brightly lit society. He has been published in *Thuglit, Shotgun Honey, Near to the Knuckle, Flash Fiction Offensive*, and various other magazines and anthologies. He has a short story collection *Down In The Devil Hole* available from *Gritfiction Ltd.* and you can find links to all of his published work at *Straightrazorfiction.com*

Kathleen A. Ryan

Kathleen A. Ryan is a retired 21-year veteran of the Suffolk County Police Department on Long Island, NY. A Macavity and Derringer Awards finalist, Kathleen writes short crime fiction and memoir. The president of Long Island Sisters in Crime (SinC), Kathleen is also a member of NY/TriState SinC, NY Mystery Writers Association, Public Safety Writers Association and Short Mystery Fiction Society. Kathleen lives with her family in Setauket, NY. www.kathleenaryan.com. She can be found on Twitter and Instagram @katcop13.

Kurt Newton

Kurt Newton's poetry has appeared in numerous publications including *Weird Tales, Mythic Delirium, Dreams and Nightmares*, and *A Sea of Alone: Poems for Alfred Hitchcock.* His eighth poetry collection *The Ultimate perVERSEities* was published in 2010. He lives in Connecticut.

Laura R. Becherer

Laura R. Becherer is an American student attending the University of Glasgow's doctorate of fine arts program. She holds a bachelor's degree in English Literature from the University of Wisconsin-Platteville and a master's degree in creative writing from the University of Wisconsin-Eau Claire. Her previous publications include an experimental nonfiction essay in the online literary journal *Atlas and Alice* and a short fiction piece in the Glasgow Women's Library publication *Sex between the covers*. She currently lives in Glasgow with her two American cats.

Leroy B. Vaughn

Leroy B. Vaughn is a retired law enforcement officer living in Arizona, USA. He has written over forty short stories that have appeared in print magazines, e-zines, pod-casts and in one newspaper.

Michael W. Clark

Michael W. Clark is a biologist and writer with thirty one short stories published. Most recently, stories have been in *Lost Souls, Surprising Stories, Trembles, Morpheus Tales* and in UC Berkeley's *Imaginarium, Death Throes, Black Heart, Tracers* and the anthology - *Fat Zombies, Creature Stew, Gumshoe Mysteries*, and *Detectives of the Fantastic*.

Nell Pates

Nell Pates is a twenty-six year old writer of fiction. She is especially interested in the theme of motivation - focusing on how context can lead a character to make the choices they do - and always attempts to explore this in her work. She left the British Army in 2015 with a view to pursuing a career as a writer. She mainly writes novels, though she has been known to try her hand at play-writing and short stories, too.

Olga Dermott-Bond

Olga Dermott-Bond is originally from Northern Ireland, studied for an M.A. in English Literature at St Andrews University, and now lives in Warwickshire with her husband and two daughters. She was Warwick Poet Laureate in 2010, and was commissioned to write for the *Poetry on Loan* scheme. She teaches English and Drama, and enjoys all kinds of creative writing.

Robert White

For the last dozen or so years, Robert White has been writing and publishing noir, hardboiled, and mainstream fiction. He has two hardboiled private-eye novels featuring series character Thomas Haftmann, one collection of short stories, and a crime novel, *When You Run with Wolves*. Also published recently is an ebook Special Collections, winner of the New Rivers Electronic Book Competition in 2014. His latest crime story online is *Queen of Hearts* in Pulpwood Fiction. White's most recent crime novel *Waiting on a Bridge of Maggots* was published in Autumn 2015 by Grand Mal Press.

Sue Iles-Jonas

For many years Sue was a criminologist working for the criminal justice system. Although she has now left the dark side and is a clinical hypnotherapist she finds time to write crime fiction in the form of short stories and she has just completed the final edit on her first novel *A Bunch of Lies*. She is a member of West Sussex Writers and has found some success with her comedy noir combo in Sussex open mics and club competitions. Her second novel will be a tale of female revenge.

✪

Jo Young

Jo Young is a mum to two young boys, who are her partners in crime. They have taught her everything she knows about hiding evidence, shifting blame and creating a diversion. She served with the British Army for seventeen years working in Canada, Cyprus, Germany, Afghanistan and the USA as well as assorted market towns in the English Home Counties. In 2015 Jo graduated with Distinction from the University of Glasgow's Creative Writing Masters programme. She continues to serve with the Army Reserve while wrestling with the novel in her bottom drawer and writing poetry inspired by her experiences. A true Yorkshire-woman, she won't be happy until she moves back to the White Rose

County in order to moan about all the stuff that used to be better before she moved away…

Sandra Kohls

Sandra Kohls went to Poland for a year in 1998 to teach English and returned to Scotland twelve years later. She has worked in so many countries that her feet can no longer be called itchy, though they still tingle occasionally. Before abduction by the travel bug, she was a waitress, a barmaid, a cook, and a bookkeeper, sold oil paintings door-to-door and pumped petrol, thus meeting enough crooked characters to last a lifetime of stories. Her writing has been featured in *From Glasgow to Saturn, Flashflood* and *Landmarks: the 2015 National Flash-Fiction Day anthology*. When not writing or working, she swims up and down her local pool making up vengeful tales about people who do doggie paddle in the fast lane. In 2015 she graduated with merit from the University of Glasgow's Creative Writing Masters programme and is writing her first novel.